STYX & STONES

AN EROTIC UNDERWORLD ROMANCE

JANUARY FOXX

ECHO BOOKS

1

Hades is hotter than I imagined.

Rogue raven hair. Eyes as black and mysterious as night. Body, as muscled and masculine as it is graceful and effortless, draped across the leather armchair across from me like a cat in the sun.

"You're a long way from home, Persephone," he purrs.

The way he says my name sends a rush of heat through me. I swallow, wondering how he knows it's me. My fingers skim the edge of the ornate mask covering the top half of my face to ensure it hasn't slipped.

It hasn't.

The dark, glittery fabric hugs the bridge of my nose, comes to theatrical points above the corners of my eyes, and is secured with a ribbon that ties beneath the top layer of my strawberry hair. It's no different from the ones worn by countless others who crowded onto the ferry earlier this evening with champagne flutes in hand and gold coins in their pockets. The same type of coin that I found in the bottom of my wine glass at a bar across town two weeks earlier. The twist of fate that set this entire evening in motion.

I'd been meeting up with friends, which was nothing out of the ordinary. A girl like me was always meeting up with friends. What else was there to do with privileged youth? Tuesdays were for trendy tapas downtown. Thursdays were for late summer biergartens near the river. Weekends were a blur of brunch, and boozy bike rides, and bookstores. This is the life that had been laid out for me, and it was the equivalent of a sunny romp through a field of four-leaf clover, like I'd been plucked from a charmed, Kelly green patch of it.

Lucky.

It's a word often used to describe me. Working class women might whisper it in reverently envious tones, but it takes on a mocking drawl when uttered by my high society peers, the same way you might roll your eyes at the friend who inherits a fortune right after winning the lottery. Because *of course* good things happen to me. Good things always happen to me. I come from a good family, have the kind of career you only get with good connections, and enjoy a long line of perfectly good guys who want to date me. There's a good chance I'll be engaged to one of them before my twenty-seventh birthday next spring.

And yet... when I plucked the gold coin from the bottom of my wine glass, my heart fluttered into my throat, and for the first time in a long time, I questioned all of it.

The string lights of the outdoor restaurant stretched across a late summer sky that had just settled into the color of over washed denim, all soft and navy, and my friends had wandered toward the bar. When I glanced over my shoulder to see if any of them had witnessed my discovery, I was relieved to find they were still arguing over whose turn it was to pay the tab.

Everything about the scene around me was entirely typical. Small groups chatted, servers buzzed from table to table, the high notes of laughter and easy indie pop carried on the breeze. Nobody nearby was interested enough to notice the flush creeping up my neck or how the tips of my ears had turned pink with excitement. And no one seemed close enough to have tampered with my drink.

But clearly, someone had.

I dropped my gaze to the coin in my hand and smoothed my thumb across the imprint, as if I needed to feel the ridges of the two-pronged spear in order for my brain to accept what my eyes were seeing.

I'd heard whispers of these tokens. The parties they gave people access to. The world they opened up. And all the things it was rumored that good girls like me gave up in the process.

Their bodies.

Their inhibitions.

Their *souls*.

I swallowed hard, as if the possibilities had formed a lump in my throat. I knew that I was not the kind of girl who would ever flock to the ferry with the masked revelers, dressed in glitter or silks or leather. It was delusional to imagine—with my reputation, my family name, and my generally sunny, wholesome disposition—that I could be. Anonymous. Reckless. Ready to slip into the shadows and indulge every dark desire. Yet when I heard my friends calling me across the restaurant, I slipped the gold disc into my top anyway.

For the rest of that evening, the warmth of the token against my skin was simultaneously reassuring and unsettling. I was horrified for anyone to find out I had it. I was terrified that I might lose it. By the time I got home, the imprint of the spear was pressed into the alabaster swell of my breast. Like some ancient sculptor had tattooed it there, right above my heart, which flailed like a caged bird in my chest as I played with the gold between my fingers.

For a few days, I kept it with me wherever I went, tucked beneath my clothes like a scandalous secret. At first, it gave me a giddy boost of confidence. By the end of the week, I had slipped toward self-loathing and considered throwing it into the river.

But I couldn't.

Some deep, dark part of me buzzed with insatiable need. My imagination frolicked through fantasies that were intended to satisfy my sexual appetite but only fueled my curiosity. In the absence of knowing exactly what the parties entailed, my desire grew wild and wanton. I imagined being held hostage, gagged and bound in a filthy dungeon. I daydreamed about being handcuffed to a table with my legs spread wide like a feast. I wondered more than once what it would be like to join one of those rumored palace orgies. With each new scenario, my pussy throbbed with forbidden longing.

It was the dreams that wore me down. The ones filled with dimly lit rooms and men who ravaged me until I was drenched, and delirious, and panting. More than one night, I woke to the force of my climax pulsing between my legs, washing me with waves of pleasure, making me desperate for *more*.

Now, standing in this library, the way Hades's hungry gaze trails down the black silk dress cupping my breasts and clinging to my hips gives me the impression that he can sense all of this. This existential unraveling. The intense desideratum. Even behind the mask, I feel exposed. Even in this long, flowy dress, far more conservative than many I've seen tonight—particularly when one considers that I'm still *wearing* it—I feel naked.

"I think you have me confused with someone else," I offer.

I try to keep an innocent smirk on my lips and my tone demurring, but the way my pulse thuds in my throat threatens to give me away. My better instincts are screaming that I shouldn't be here. At the very least, I should have left when the guests started trading their champagne for party drugs and shedding their formalwear in favor of sensual stretches of skin, begging to be touched. I shouldn't have escaped to this secluded library and locked myself inside, only to find myself alone with the handsome host.

"I think I may," Hades muses in his smooth, smoky voice. "The girl I'm thinking of would never have crossed the river if she knew what goes on over here. Then again, maybe she would have. Maybe she's secretly desperate to know what happens to good girls who wander too far from home."

His words tighten through me, tugging deep and low in my belly, spreading the fire that has been under my skin since I got here. Maybe it's shame that burns through me. Maybe it's desire. Maybe it's some intoxicating mixture of both—the same cocktail I've been nursing every day since I found that coin, during those stolen moments where I would slip my fingers into my panties and massage my swollen clit until waves of pleasure rocked through me. Each time I wanted to know: what would it be like to cash in that token and find myself standing right *here*?

Here, with books lining the shelves, a fire crackling in the hearth, and the muffled sounds of music and moans and every depraved fantasy audible through the heavy wooden door.

"I was actually just leaving."

I can't tell if it's a lie, because I make no attempt to head toward the exit. I'm held in place by the intense stare of this impossibly sexy man, whose gaze is currently edging along the slit in my dress that runs all the way up one thigh, like I secretly wish his fingers would.

"You aren't enjoying the party?"

His accent is more pronounced now, or maybe I've finally calmed down enough to notice it. I can't place it, but it feels at once familiar and foreign. And dangerously seductive.

"It's... not what I expected," I admit. Another half-truth.

Did I expect anything I've seen here tonight? The way some people caress and explore each other in the way one savors good food, reverent and slow. The way that others greedily ripped at clothes and claimed partners like prey, leaving shreds of fabric and screams in their wake. And then there were those interactions that fell somewhere in between, like discovering that the captivating woman with whom I'd shared a polite drink on the ferry was bent over a buffet table with a god-like man thrusting into her from behind, while he doled out both physical punishment and murmured praise as she hungrily attempted to fit two hard, eager cocks into her mouth at once.

My well-bred propriety had warred with carnal desire. It was enthralling, and yet I couldn't watch—could I? I found myself retreating down one hallway, then another, before choosing the heavy wooden door at random. When I closed it behind me, I'd been so relieved to find this room full of books. I've always felt at home among books, but this time they don't promise escape. Not entirely.

The sound of the scene I left behind is burned into my brain. The slap of skin on skin. The slick, wet noises that accompanied the juices dripping down the woman's thighs and neck and chin. The low, desperate, muffled moan like she was begging for more even though so much of her was already stretched full.

"You didn't expect to see people taking their pleasure from each other so freely, or you didn't expect to like it?"

I sink my teeth into my bottom lip, unsure of how to answer this. I'm aware of my own arousal, hot and slick between my legs as I shift on my feet.

"Both," I admit.

Hades smiles, if you could call it that. The edge of his beautiful mouth barely ticks upward, the corners of his eyes imperceptibly crease. By any normal standards, this wouldn't be called a smile, but the overall effect is one of satisfaction.

He stands now, crossing to a small bar cart and pouring himself a lowball of amber liquid from a decanter. With his back to me, I dare to drink in more of him.

His dark, impeccably tailored clothes. His tall frame and broad shoulders. The easy grace with which he moves, like a practiced predator. Am I his prey?

"Anyone here is free to leave whenever they like. This is a party, not a hostage situation. If you decide at this moment to walk out the door, head back to the ferry, and return to your pretty life, no one will stop you." He turns, pausing to assess me over the rim of his glass. "But if you do, you'll spend the rest of your life wondering what might have happened if you stayed and had a drink with me."

I want to scoff and tell him he's wrong, but the hungry feeling under my skin screams that he's right. It's been haunting me for days, how I can't quite sate this urge.

"And what will happen?" I manage. "If I stay and have this drink."

The fire casts dancing shadows across his chiseled cheekbones as he studies me. "What do you want to happen?"

This feels like an invitation, and my body responds. Goosebumps spread across my skin and my nipples harden. I wonder if he can see them through the thin fabric of my dress.

My response comes quieter this time. "I don't know."

When he passes me a glass, I hug it with both hands to give them something to do, and I drop my focus to the liquid, wondering if I'm really going to drink it.

This is stranger danger.

This is everything they tell you not to do at a party.

Within a moment, a single finger snugs beneath my chin and lifts my gaze to meet his. This close, I see that his eyes aren't black, they're blue. Blue like the ocean at night: deep, and beautiful, and terrifying.

He moves the pad of his finger across the part of my lips, pressing gently. "If you're going to stay, I'll ask that you stick to the truth."

My lips part instinctively, grazing them against his touch as I nod. He nods in unison, tracing a gentle line along my jaw, down my neck, edging beneath the thin strap of my top and lingering there, like he's considering slipping it over my shoulder.

He doesn't. And it kills me. Every nerve in my body wants him to keep touching me. To touch more of me.

"Why did you come here, Persephone?"

The fire crackles in the expectant silence. I lift the proffered glass to my lips and take a long, slow gulp. I expected whiskey, but it's closer to rum: spicy, and honeyed, and decadent. It warms through my chest, lacing my veins with the last bit of bravery I need. I tongue the sweetness off my lips.

"I'm tired of being good."

2

Satisfaction seeps into his features at my admission. The glimmer of his smile is wicked as he steps closer. He's so close my nose brushes his bottom lip, and I have to tip my head to look him in the eye.

"I don't think you're good," he says slowly. "I think you're a dirty girl whose pussy is so wet that all she can think about is how much she wants me to take off her dress and make her do things she would never admit she wants to do."

My shuddering exhale falls across his mouth.

"Fuck," I breathe.

It's only then that I realize I'm trembling. Is it with fear? Desire? Anticipation? Everything about being here has confused my senses.

"Oh, my sweet little nymph," he purrs. "I'm talking about so much more than fucking. But you have to agree to a few ground rules."

"Which are?"

"No hiding," he says. "You'll take off this dress. You'll take off your mask. And you'll stop pretending you're some delicate, greenhouse flower. You'll have to own your part in this."

He smooths a hand up my waist, and I instinctively press further into his touch. His hands accept this as an invitation to rove. He traces the teardrop curve of one breast, letting his thumb find the hard peak of my nipple through the fabric. He flicks it up and down, sending another aching jolt of need through me.

A reply works its way up my throat. "Okay."

He smirks, and his movements become lazy and languid, like he's purposely avoiding the most sensitive parts of me. He drags his fingers between the swell of my breasts.

"And you'll address me as sir."

A sensual smile plays across my lips. "Yes, *sir*. Anything else?"

"You'll become mine to use as I please. If I want to fuck you, I'll fuck you. If I want to share you, I'll share you. I can pleasure you or deny you or discipline you. You'll give me whatever I want, without hesitation. And in exchange I'll give you what you want. Things you don't even know you want. I'll worship your greedy cunt like a goddess. And I won't stop until I've pushed you past the edge of absolute oblivion."

My pulse throbs in my throat, between my legs. I swallow hard.

"What if I can't take it?" I venture. "What if it's too much?"

"Then say the word, and everything stops. You can leave and go home. I told you, I don't take hostages here."

I bite my lower lip, wondering if now is the time to bring up that I've heard differently. Everyone's heard the rumors about the girls who venture across the river Styx and don't come back.

Kidnapped, they say.

Sex slaves, they whisper.

He puts distance between us now, moving to drape himself back over the chair as if he doesn't care one way or the other whether I stay or go. He tips his glass to his mouth.

I fight the urge to settle across his lap with my dress pushed up around my hips. Would I feel his own desire pressing hard against me? Does he need this as much as I do?

"What's the word?" I question.

"Whatever you want it to be. Something you wouldn't say in normal conversation, but something you'll remember."

A safe word, my brain supplies. I've never done anything with anyone that requires a safe word. It seems to imply that I'm putting myself in a situation that is decidedly *un*safe. But I want this, and not just because I'm horny as hell. The attraction I feel for Hades is an all-consuming, soul-tugging magnetism that begs my boundaries to blur.

"Olympus," I say.

He makes a tsk-tsk sound. "I guess there's no place like home, is there, princess?"

"With all due respect, *sir*, I'm no princess."

"Maybe you'd like to be my whore, then? Assuming we have a deal."

The offer stretches between us. A beat passes. Two. Any more and I know I'll overthink it.

I slip the straps of my dress over my shoulders and guide the fabric down until it catches on my hips. When I roll them slowly from side to side, the black silk pools at my feet with a gentle swish. The light from the fire dances across my bare breasts, accentuates the curve of my waist, glistens across the wetness between my thighs.

Hades notices my arousal in a way that makes me feel like he'd love to lick it off. When I imagine him kneeling on the rug before me, with his face buried between my legs, another wave of wanting spreads through me. Is that what he meant by worshiping me? How long until I find out?

When his gaze trails up, I'm aware that my mask is still in place. A single, silky ribbon is the only thing still tethering me to the outside world. The only thing standing between me and the Underworld.

I take a long drink from my glass, finishing it in three gulps and leaving it empty on the nearest shelf. I let its hazy warmth sear through my chest, tingle down to the tips of my toes. Then I thread my fingers into my hair and tug the ribbon loose.

The mask falls away. A blush heats my unobscured face.

When Hades inclines his head toward the flames, I hesitate. I see him track this, and I wonder if he'll punish me for it later. I look down at the form-fitting disguise and hear his voice in my head.

No hiding.

No hesitation.

And in exchange...

There's no going back from here. As soon as I say yes, I'll have given myself up to him. And the moment I step out that door, everyone will know who I am.

With a flick of my wrist, I toss the mask into the fire. The flames consume it with a flare, hot and fast and hungry. I drag my defiant gaze back to where he's waiting.

"We have a deal," I say.

Hades motions me closer with a single finger. When I get within reach, he takes my hands and places them on the back of the chair, over either side of his shoulders.

"Good," he murmurs. "Keep them there."

"Okay," I say.

The position leaves me leaning forward with my breasts only inches from his face. They swell and sway with my attempts at a steadying breath.

His gaze flicks up to mine. "That wasn't a question."

He uses his knee to widen my stance and smooths a hand up the wetness of my inner thigh, meeting my arousal with a deep hum of satisfaction.

"Such a horny little nymph," he says, grazing his knuckles across my swollen clit. "You want it so bad, don't you? This pleasure you're so ashamed of."

"Yes," I manage. I barely recognize my own voice. My words are little more than a saccharine sigh.

"Yes what?" he prompts.

"Yes, sir."

He increases the pressure, sliding his knuckles up and down my slick center. Parting my lips. Teasing my opening. Drawing a slow line all the way back to the sweetness of Venus before withdrawing his touch.

I whimper in response, desperate to follow.

"We'll get to that," he says. "But first we need to formalize our arrangement."

He reaches for an ornate wooden box on the small end table beside his chair. When he flips it open, I catch glimpses of a rich satin lining, and black leather, and the glint of something shiny. My heart speeds to a gallop.

Instinctively, I start to pull back. Maybe it's nerves. Maybe it's to get a better look, or prepare for what's to come. Either way, it's a mistake. Hades snatches my wrist and guides it back to the chair. There's a sense of finality in the movement that tells me he'll only tolerate correcting me once. His mouth catches the sensitive skin of my inner forearm with a gentle nip of teeth, followed by a stroke of his tongue.

"Are you going to be a problem, Persephone?" he asks.

"No, sir."

"Patience is a virtue," he purrs. "And you, my pet, are going to learn it. Among other things."

I close my eyes and release a small, shaky sigh. "I'm sorry. I'm a little nervous."

"Good. It'll make this more fun."

I swallow hard, turning my safe word over in the back of my mind the same way I played that coin between my fingers before getting on the ferry. But, like the token, I know I can only use it once. And I'm too curious about what's in that box to use it now.

"Nervousness is just a state of heightened awareness. It's a type of—"

Hades pauses to wrap something buttery soft around the column of my throat. Or, at least, the part that's touching my neck is soft. I realize once he's fastening the buckle that the outside is stiff like leather.

"—arousal," he concludes.

He hooks two fingers beneath it to make sure it's snug but not too tight. Heat licks through me.

"A collar," I say.

"So everyone knows you belong to me. This is my house. I make the rules. And with this, no one will touch you without my permission. Unless they have a death wish."

I'm desperate to inspect it with my fingers, but I make do with shifting my head a little side-to-side, testing its fit.

His gaze dances across my face. "What are you thinking?"

No hiding.

"I think I want to touch it," I murmur. "And I think it's kind of... hot. Really fucking hot."

"Have you ever fantasized about wearing a collar before?"

I bite my bottom lip, wondering if it's going to be swollen soon from how much I've been worrying it with my teeth.

"Yes," I admit.

"And what did you do in this fantasy, while you had it on?"

My face burns. "Got down on my hands and knees. And begged."

He runs a coaxing hand up the smooth plane of my belly, and it takes every bit of my concentration to keep still.

"Begged for what?"

I force the words out slowly. "To get spanked. And spread open. And fucked hard."

This is the right answer, because he cups my breasts, kneading them until I moan at the relief of the contact. He teases my nipples with featherlight flicks. My fingers grip the leather chairback in an effort to keep myself from melting against him.

"You could have done any of those things out there," he says, nodding toward the door. "So why did you come in here?"

The truth dances just out of reach.

I was looking for the exit, the good girl in me defends. *I got turned around.*

"I came in here to..."

My baser self laughs in my ear. *You came in here to touch yourself. To rub that horny ache between your thighs until you moaned like a whore and sent yourself over the edge, like you've been doing every chance you get for the past two weeks.*

I blush at the thought. It felt wrong being out there with the rest of the party, but I can't deny it turned me on. I knew I couldn't last another minute without release.

A sudden slap stings across my left breast. I yelp out a cry.

"The truth, princess," he prompts.

"To get myself off," I say in a rush. "I came in here to be alone and get myself off."

I feel him smile against my skin, where the sensation of his mouth mingles with the lingering pain of his repri-mand. He soothes the sting with his tongue, trailing kisses across the fullness of my breast until he finds the eager peak. I let out a long, low moan of relief as he sucks it into his mouth.

"Ohhh my god," I murmur.

He pinches my other nipple, rolling it between his fingers.

"See? Was that so hard?" he teases, licking me.

I don't know how to answer this. Every movement of his mouth is making me drunk with pleasure. I want to run my fingers through his hair, but I settle for digging my fingernails into the furniture.

"I'm just new to this."

"Something tells me you're not new to this at all," he says. "Something tells me you've wanted it for a long, *long* time. That you've thought about it every time some boy, who likes to pretend he's a man, sticks his cock in you and still manages to leave you disappointed. Because he doesn't know that *this* is really what you want."

I realize that every lick and bite he's bestowing on my tits is tugging at my clit, like all the nerve endings are tethered together. His innate knowledge of my body—the way he explores without rushing, as if there is no greater goal than his mouth on my skin and his name on my lips—is even more irresistible than his disarmingly handsome features.

"Is it okay to say that I want you?" I sigh. "Because I want you. Really, fucking, bad."

"Patience, Persephone. First, I get what I want. Then, you get what you want."

"What do you want?"

"I want to play with your gorgeous tits until you come."

"I don't know if I can—" I attempt to catch my breath. "—come like this."

"We'll have to see about that, won't we?" He teases with his teeth before licking gently, switching off between each breast in a skilled rhythm. "It's part of your training. I need to see how you respond. What you're capable of."

I begin to wonder exactly where that line will be drawn. He nurses my need until the pleasure borders on pain, then switches to gentle caresses, then alternates sides. His movements are intuitive, always changing up at the precise moment one touch borders on too much. It's the difference between holding a sour candy in one single spot on your tongue versus expertly moving it around so that you can savor every last bit without succumbing to the burn.

And savoring it I am. Every lick. Every touch. The way he bites, and sucks, and teases. I realize he's layering my pleasure, one sensation on top of the other, and with each new level my desperation builds.

The slithering clink of metal brings me back to myself. I've only registered that he's rummaging through the box when the soft, plastic ends of a clamp pinch tight around one nipple.

Very tight.

An unexpected whimper escapes me, and my palms almost leave the chair. I press into them harder.

I don't know what I expect. Definitely not the jolt of pleasure that surges through me as he tugs to test its grip.

"Fuck," I swear.

My clit is so swollen it feels like a slick, ripe fruit, ready to be eaten, and it twitches each time he touches the clamp. I'm making little mewling noises with each of his movements.

"Breathe," he coaxes.

I do. He rubs the exposed tip of the sensitive bud. I shudder another moaning sigh.

"Do you want the other one?"

I can't believe my own voice. The words slip out before I can think them. "Yes, please."

"Mmm, already begging. I like that about you. You're so—" He fastens the second clamp, and a feral sound escapes me. "—eager."

The sound of metal on metal shifts as he clips something to my collar. I half-expect a leash, but then the cool chains settle in the valley between my breasts and swoop back to the point where my nipples are pinched tight. When he gives them a tentative tug, I tip dangerously close to climax, and I realize this shimmery chain isn't jewelry. Hades is the puppet master of my own pleasure, pulling strings to see which combination makes me come alive.

"Now that you're mine, I want to be clear on a few things."

He works the chains in alternating tugs, and I murmur something incoherent in response.

"You only get to come when I want you to come. If I catch you sneaking off to pleasure yourself again, there will be consequences."

Urgent heat spreads through me like fire, pooling molten and liquid between my legs. They're trembling, and I realize despite my earlier protests that I'm right at the edge. It doesn't make sense. He's teasing my tits, but it's my pussy that responds, almost as if that's the part of me he's been toying with this entire time.

"Do we understand each other, pet?"

I try to hold his gaze, but I can barely keep my eyes from rolling up to the ceiling, as if begging for deliverance.

"Permission to come now, sir?"

This is a courtesy, a flimsy attempt on my part to play by the rules, but my climax is imminent whether he says yes or not.

"I thought you said you couldn't come like this. I thought you said you needed *more*."

He leans forward and flicks the firm tip of his tongue across my pinched nipples, but it feels like he's licking my clit, hard and fast. The pleasure is incomprehensible.

"I'm... I can't... stop..." Every muscle in my body is wound tight. I grit my teeth. "Holy fuck, please."

He teases me with his dark voice like a man taunting a dog, tugging at its chains. "You want to come? Does my good horny nymph want to come?"

"Yes, fuck, I'm—"

Release consumes me, and nothing has ever felt this good. It feels like waking up from one of my wet dreams, with pleasure pulsing between my legs and my pussy clenching around nothing, begging to be stroked and filled up.

"That's it," he coaxes.

He spreads his hands wide over my hips to hold me up as I ride it out, punctuating my moans by removing the clamps and gently sucking at the soreness.

"Oh my god, I'm still..."

"Yes," he murmurs against my skin. "Come for me, princess."

With the last of it, my knees give way. My entire body feels boneless, all raw nerve endings and aftershocks of pleasure.

Hades tucks me against his chest and drapes my trembling legs over his lap, and I whimper with relief as I finally get to touch him. With my nose nuzzled against his neck, I realize he smells like a late night fire. I want it to consume me.

He strokes down the outline of my body as he holds me. I can't make sense of this. Hades—the keeper of souls, the maker of deals, the devil himself—is *holding* me. Caressing me. For a moment, I question if this is another one of my depraved dreams.

I dare to trail my fingers into his hair and press a tentative kiss against his jaw for proof of life. I don't know if this is allowed. When he doesn't stop me, I get bolder. In a few languid movements I shift until we're front-to-front. He reaches up and tucks a swath of long hair behind my ear, before trailing his fingers along the edge of my collar. His eyes sparkle with lust.

"Have you had enough yet, my pet? Or are you ready for more?"

I roll my hips until I feel the hard length of his erection straining against his black pants, pressing between my legs, and holy *fuck*. He's big, and thick, and ready. This knowledge sends a fresh surge of need through me.

I lean forward until my nose brushes his, until I'm sliding my hands up his chest and gathering his shirt into fistfuls that tug the tail ends from his beltline. When he doesn't stop me, I frame his strong jaw with my fingers, tipping his mouth within a millimeter of mine. He waits with barely a breath between us, and I can't decide if the way his gaze holds mine is a challenge or an invitation. I'm wondering if I dare to kiss death in the same moment I lean in and taste him.

His full bottom lip. His top. The parted crease of them, which widens as his tongue meets mine with a teasing flick, drawing me deeper, and deeper, until he can swallow the tiny sighs that I string between each caress. Hades kisses with that same slow, sensual confidence that I'm coming to crave. I can't get enough. I wonder, when it comes to him, if there ever could be enough.

When we finally break apart, his lips twitch into a grin. "More it is."

3

When I decided to come here, I told my family I was staying with friends for the weekend, and I told my friends I was staying with family. It occurs to me as I lie across the Scheele green chaise longue near the open window, with a pashmina draped across the valley between my hip and my shoulder, that nobody will be any the wiser if I don't come home tonight. Not until Monday, actually. Even then, if I don't show up to one of the dozens of community garden projects I manage across the city, it could take days for the people who actually run the day-to-day operations to realize I'm not there.

For such an 'important person', I'm remarkably expendable. I can't tell if the thought comforts or haunts me.

I watch Hades add another log to the fire and catch hints of jasmine drifting in on the breeze. The late summer air hints of fall, shifting across the velvet curtains like the sensual sway of a woman's skirt. My gaze drifts to my own discarded dress, lying in a shadowy heap in the middle of the library floor. I regard it like a skin I might have shed: a husk of the woman I was before I set foot on this side of the Styx.

It's a delicate balance, people like to say, between my world and this one. Why rush? Everyone makes it to this side eventually, if you believe in that sort of thing. There's a time in everyone's life when negotiations must be made and bargains must be struck.

But I know not everyone experiences *this*. When fates are weighed and good deeds can no longer go unpunished, most people are sent elsewhere. If that conspiracy-theorist Dante is to be believed, some of them wind up in the layers and layers of earth that have been carved out beneath us, trapped like canaries in a mineshaft with no one to hear the warning. Some linger along the banks of the other rivers of the underworld, drowning in their own woes or lamenting what could have been. It's generally believed, though, that the majority of those who cross over enjoy a much-needed rest.

But none of those places are *here*. This palatial estate—with its endless rooms, decadent furniture, and sprawling gardens—belongs only to Hades, and the people here are only those who have been invited.

"Did you leave that coin for me?" I ask.

I prop my head into my hand and watch him poke at the flames in the hearth with an iron rod.

"You know I don't cross the river."

"That's not really an answer, is it?" I retort.

With the warm light dancing across his face, it's hard to tell if he smirks, but I hear it in his voice. "No, it isn't. And yes, I did. In a manner of speaking."

"Why?"

He lifts the crystal stopper off the decanter and pours another round of drinks before moving to sit in the space next to the arm of the chair. I adjust so that I can rest my head in his lap, looking up at him as his fingers play in my hair.

He takes a long, thoughtful draw from his glass. "In my line of work, it pays to know things. And I know a lot about you."

I give him a coy smile. "Plenty of people think they know me."

"And yet no one knows you're here."

This stills something within me. How could he possibly know this?

He must read the shift in my expression, because he adds, "That's not a threat, little nymph. You only have to say the word, and I'll send you across the river, safe and sound. I'm only suggesting that those people don't know you as well as you like to pretend."

I know, especially after tonight, that what he's saying feels like an undeniable truth.

"Why did you bring me here?"

"I can't *bring* anyone here. Freewill, and the Fates, and all that. I can only *invite*."

"The Fates. They're real?"

He waves a hand. "They're three old house cats, batting around balls of yarn. You don't have to worry about them."

"Because I'm here," I reason. "With you."

"Yes."

I let this sink in. Or at least, I attempt to. I probably need a drink.

When I reach for the glass from my reclining position, some of its contents spill across the fabric of the chaise. The mistake jolts me upright.

"Oh!" I quickly wipe at the stain. "I'm sorry. I didn't mean to—"

Hades retrieves the glass from my hand with ease and uses his other to settle me back against his lap.

"Relax," he insists. "Allow me."

He dips two fingers into the liquid and drags them over my bottom lip, down my chin, between my breasts.

"*Oh*," I sigh.

My eyes roll closed, and the fire crackles as he dips into the glass again. This time, when he spreads the honeyed liquor across my lips, I draw him into my mouth and suck the sweetness off.

His groan catches me off guard, and my lids slide open to find him watching me, all shadows and lust. He withdraws, tracing the edge of my collar.

"You're beautiful," he murmurs. "Like stepping outside after a long winter and realizing it's spring."

After everything else he's said to me so far this evening, this phrase brings a blush into my cheeks.

When he wets his fingers again, he hovers them above my lips so that I have to reach for him. I crane my neck, but he moves a tiny bit further away. He prevents me from bridging the gap by widening it again, and again, until I'm frustrated enough to snag his fingers with my teeth. A pleasurable hum vibrates in his throat when I wrap my lips around him, drawing them deeper with my tongue, mimicking the gentle suction I wish I could apply to the part of him that is growing hard beneath me, aroused by this little game.

"Is that why you invited me?" I ask.

"So many questions," he teases. "Makes me think your mouth isn't quite full enough."

This time, he doesn't bother with his hands. He holds the glass above my lips and carefully tips it. Amber liquid trickles into my open mouth, across my tongue. When I pause to swallow, he doesn't stop, simply trails the dribble down my chin, my throat, across my breasts. The rivulets are cool against my skin, leaving goosebumps in their wake.

The sound that escapes me falls somewhere between a sigh and a laugh.

"You're making a mess."

"I am," he agrees.

He slides the pashmina over my hip and sends it into the floor. He repositions until he can pour liquor down my belly, into the hollows just above my hips, over the mound of my sex. I gasp as the chill runs between my legs, contrasting my own heat.

"Somebody," he purrs, "should probably clean this up."

When the glass is empty, he sinks to his knees. He licks the trail between my breasts, down my stomach, to the thimble sized shot that has settled into my navel. By the time he positions himself between my thighs, I'm protesting before I can catch myself.

"You don't have to do this."

This is a standard line. I've probably said it to every boyfriend who has ever made a compulsory effort at oral pleasure. They usually look sheepishly grateful when I give them an easy out, eager to write this off as something I don't like and adhere to my wishes. At this knee-jerk statement, Hades's eyes flicker with something else.

He spreads his hand wide, pressing the heel hard against my sex and dragging it up my lower belly, until he can grip the small of my waist.

"I think you've forgotten yourself, little nymph. I don't do anything I don't want to do. And I want your greedy cunt in my face."

Heat spreads through me—in my burning cheeks, in my still swollen clit, in my already throbbing pussy.

I suck in a breath. "Yes, sir."

He hooks my knees over his shoulders and drags my hips to the very end of the chair.

"Still not a question, princess."

I giggle in response, but it's quickly replaced by a deeper, breathier sound as his mouth meets me.

"Mmm. You taste like honey."

I know it's likely the liquor, but it lights me up anyway. I suddenly feel sweet, and savory, and worthy of being devoured. But Hades takes his time. Dipping his tongue across my opening. Circling my clit. I find myself rolling my hips to meet his mouth, opening for him wider, and feeling his hum of approval against me.

"You are scary good at this," I breathe.

I feel him smile just before he catches his teeth around my clit, holding it in place while he tongues the sensitive center like a juicy pomegranate seed.

I dare to thread a hand through his hair, gripping the glossy silk strands between my fingers as I writhe against him, as he coaxes me toward the edge. It's easier this time to slip toward it. This pleasure is more familiar. He circles the bud the same way I imagined I was going to when I retreated in here, with my dress around my hips and my fingers slick with my own arousal.

I'm almost at my tipping point when he pulls back.

I paw at him. "Wait. No. I'm so—"

He bites the inside of my thigh, quick but hard enough to leave a mark. I finish my sentence with a stifled yelp.

"What was that?" he asks.

I suck my lips between my teeth, trying to quiet the urge to drag him against me and beg. My hips roll against nothing, eager for friction and finding only air.

I attempt to rephrase. "I was close to coming."

"I know." He nuzzles against me, and I whimper. "I don't want you to come yet."

I thrust my head back against the cushion in frustration, gripping the collar with both hands and wondering if this is my own personal hell.

But no, I know from the way that pleasure thrums through me like a bassline that it's not that at all. This feeling is too real to exist in those fantasy places. Heaven. Hell. This pleasure is too tangible: here and now.

"I want to know," he continues, teasing my opening, "all your dirty secrets. What makes you wet."

He slides one finger inside me, then two.

"What makes you beg."

He finds my most sensitive spot and hooks against it, rubbing side-to-side.

"What makes you crazy."

This, I think. This makes me crazy. But I don't dare say that out loud.

He continues his steady rhythm, fucking me with his hand.

"Which one of those things is this, Persephone?"

I lie, even though I know better. "Wet. It makes me wet."

"Hmm."

He reaches beside me and snags a throw pillow, wedging it under my ass so that my hips are angled up toward his face. He returns to his stroking, only this time the feeling is amplified.

"What about now?"

My response is a series of garbled vowels.

"Better," he says.

He ignores my clit, though it's desperate to be touched again. But this is something else entirely. It's like he's found the very roots of my pleasure, and with each movement he follows them deeper, stroking the way one does a stray cat's chin. The pressure inside me builds—along with a sensation that's more urgent.

I writhe against his touch, unsure if I'm trying to move toward it or away.

"Hades," I warn. "I'm worried I'm going to—"

"You won't."

I wonder if he even knows what I was going to say. That the pleasure has mingled with this feeling like I'm going to piss all over him. He licks up my center, and my insides clench tight around his fingers.

"I want your cock," I beg. "Please, sir, can I have your cock?"

"No," he says.

"But—"

He withdraws his hand in an instant, and suddenly he's flipping me onto my belly. His palm stings sharp blows across my ass.

One.

Two.

I gasp and whimper, but the sensation is *everything.*

Three.

"What did I fucking tell you, princess?" he asks, his accent stronger now that he's frustrated. *Wot did I focking tell you.*

I'm braced for the next blow, but this time he palms my ass and squeezes, kneading the stinging flesh. Every nerve in my body buzzes.

"Are you ready to behave?"

"Yes, sir," I breathe. "I'll behave. I'll be anything you want."

"Is that so?"

He lifts my hips until I'm propped on my shins and knees, hauling my backend high into the air as he presses the side of my face against the velvet cushions.

"I want you to be good and hold still."

I hear a zipper and sense from the shift in his breathing that he's stroking himself. For a brief, beautiful moment, I think he's going to fuck me. He rubs the thick head of his cock up and down my slick center, notching himself against my entrance. He presses against me as far as he can without giving me what I so desperately need.

"Mm. Your pussy is so fucking hot, Persephone. I can't wait to sink all the way into you. How many times do you think I'll make you come before then?"

I swear into the cushion, pressing my mouth into it to muffle the sound of my groan. I'm nearly trembling with the effort of holding still. If I shift back even a centimeter...

"That wasn't an answer."

I close my eyes and wet my lips, trying to remember how to form words.

"As many times as you want, sir."

I can hear the smile in his voice. "I think you're catching on."

Then he's gone.

My self-control breaks. I roll my hips, edging back as far as I dare, but I can't reach him. He tucks himself back into his pants. The sound of his zipper dashes my hopes. A shuddering sigh escapes me.

"Now," he says. "Let's try this again."

I hear him fumbling with something on a nearby shelf. When he returns, he's got a smooth, nubby silicon toy.

I appreciate, not for the first time, that this man has sex toys hidden in his library. He slides it up and down a few times before pressing it in. The bulb on the end of it snugs against the perfect spot. In another instant, it vibrates to life. I moan in response.

"Does it feel good, little nymph?"

"So fucking good," I manage.

After the brief absence of him, my need has doubled. Every sensation is heightened.

"Are you still worried about ruining my chair?"

I furrow my brow. "Yes."

"I don't give a fuck about the chair."

I attempt to let this reassure me, but all my muscles are wound tight. When I try to relax, my breath comes in desperate pants. I claw at the velvet cushion beneath me.

"Hades," I say.

"Sir," he corrects.

A wretched moan escapes me. "Sir, I think this is too much."

He works the toy in me harder, faster. "Is it?"

God, this feeling. It feels so, fucking, good. And yet, so impossible. I'm terrified he could hold me here forever, fighting my own orgasm until I don't have anything left.

"If you want it to stop, you know the word."

I bite down so hard into my bottom lip I'm worried it might bleed, because I *won't* say it. Not now, when I'm so very close, and if he would just –

He clicks the vibration up a notch, and actual tears well in my eyes. I growl as I grind back against him.

"You remember the word, don't you?"

My hips seem to move of their own accord, lifting higher, begging him deeper. He rocks harder against that sweet, deep ache.

"Oh fuck *yes*," I groan. When I say it, I don't even remotely think it's a response to his question.

"No, that's not it. I think it started with an O," he continues. "Ol... Om... No. Maybe... orgasm—was that it?"

I'm starting to lose my grasp of language as he fucks me with the toy.

"Yes, please," I pant.

"You want to come again?" he teases. "After I spanked you like a bad girl?"

Yes. Yes. Fuck. Yes.

I realize I'm chanting it. Screaming it.

"Fucking come for me, then."

I cry out, because I can't, I really *can't*—but I also can't hold it back anymore. With a sob, I let go. When my pussy begins to spasm, it comes from some deep well within me. Hot liquid spills down my legs.

"Oh my god, I'm—"

Squirting? All over his couch?

"—sorry," I gasp. "I'm so—"

"Don't apologize."

Hades withdraws the toy and sinks to his knees. He drags his face between my legs, nuzzling against me.

"Don't ever fucking apologize for the pleasure I give you. Do you understand?"

He licks my oversensitive pussy until I'm moaning with every breath, until every touch sends a visible jolt through me, until his face is slick with my arousal.

"Yes," I pant. "I understand. I understand!"

I gasp as he pulls away.

"Good."

My legs are trembling like a new foal as he lowers me to my belly. I melt against the chaise like butter, and he crawls over me, trailing tender kisses up the length of my spine. At the back of my neck, he smooths my hair away from the collar and removes the rogue locks stuck to my face. I don't realize there are tears until he thumbs the wetness off my cheeks.

"How do you feel?"

Spent, I think. Entirely spent.

He must read it on my face, because he gives a single, understanding nod. He helps me sit upright before finding the pashmina and draping it around my shoulders. I know I must look wrecked, but he tips my mouth up to meet his with a reverent brush of his thumb along my jaw, like I've never been more beautiful.

"Let's get you cleaned up, shall we?"

I cast a nervous glance at the door as my fingers find the comforting presence of the collar. Even though he promised the adornment means nobody will touch me without his permission, the thought of leaving this room—of stepping back out into the raucous hallways and ballrooms of the sprawling party—makes me feel so overwhelmed. Especially in my current, hyper-aroused state.

My voice is small and tentative. "Are you taking me out there?"

Relief floods me when he shakes his head. "Not tonight."

When he crosses to one of the built-in bookcases on the far wall, he pulls a volume from the shelf, and the entire panel slides open to reveal a hidden door. He inclines his head to the opening. My thighs quake with the effort of trying to stand, and despite my best attempt, I barely lift my hips off the cushion before settling right back into my seat.

"Unless," he says, "you'd rather head home."

There's no question in his tone, but there's one in the blue-black depths of his expectant gaze.

"It's not that," I admit. "I just don't think I can walk right now."

His expression softens with the glimmer of a smile. He comes and scoops me up like I weigh nothing.

"Anything else, princess?"

I loop my arms around his neck.

"My dress?" I offer, eyeing the pile on the floor.

He smirks. "You won't need it where we're going."

In a few long strides, we're slipping into the secret passageway with the door to the library clicking shut behind us.

4

The corridor is quiet with the exception of Hades's sure steps. Gas lanterns light the twisting hallways, bathing the stone walls in golden warmth. We pass door after door, all closed and unmarked, and I wonder where they lead. In fact, I wonder where any of this leads. Every turn we make looks the same.

"Is this a maze?" I ask.

"Just a shortcut," he replies.

After the next turn, we spot a trio in black servers' uniforms, smoking and laughing. The sound of clanging pots and general commotion drift through the door they've propped open with a liquor crate. Suddenly, this whole thing feels normal, like we could be passing the backdoors of the bars and restaurants I frequent back home. The ones that currently feel so very far away.

The trio sobers when they see us, but it's a respectful silence. Their spines straighten. Their eyes shine with quiet intrigue. I attempt to nestle myself deeper into Hades's arms, but the collar pinches my neck when I try to tuck my face against his chest. His mouth finds the top of my head.

"No hiding," he murmurs into my hair.

I do my best to act normal—as if being carried past strangers, naked and recently ravaged, is at all normal—but still, I'm grateful for the minimal cover of the thin pashmina as we draw closer.

Hades inclines his head, greeting them each by name. "Alex. Angel. Nick. Enjoying the evening so far?"

"Yes, sir," they offer eagerly. "Absolutely, sir."

"It's a great turnout tonight," the youngest looking server remarks with a giddy shrug. "And they're really going through the wine. Dionysus and his entourage, I mean. But we hauled up extra from the cellar when we saw them coming."

I can tell he's trying to impress, and the sideways look that the more seasoned woman cuts him indicates that she's embarrassed he's being a complete fangirl.

"Smart lad," Hades offers. "Keep up the good work."

We're only a few steps away when I begin to hear them whispering under their breath. I peek over Hades's shoulder, hiding my smile against his shirt as I watch them jab each other in the ribs and critique the interaction.

"Oh, and Nick?" Hades says.

The entire group stops their silent argument in the split second before he turns around. The newbie gets a little taller.

"Yes, sir?"

"Bring around a grazing board, if you have a moment. And some wine, assuming that shameless lush hasn't drunk it all yet. We'll be in the spa."

Nick accepts the task with resolute seriousness, as if he's just been awarded the highest honor. "Yes, sir," he nods.

We continue our trajectory, and I study the strong jaw and carved cheekbones of the man carrying me. When he turns down another path, I realize I couldn't find my way back to the library if I wanted. No use looking back now.

"The spa," I say, noting our intended destination. "Like fuzzy robes and cucumber water?"

His full lips twitch at the corner. "What kind of sadist puts cucumbers in water? No. This is a Roman spa."

"Mm," I nod. "And that's different how?"

"Patience, Persephone." Though he says it as a low, drawling command, his dark eyes twinkle with a hint of amusement.

Within the next few moments, we pause at one of the nondescript doors. In a smooth, easy flex of muscle, Hades hauls my weight over one shoulder. I yip, sure that I'm falling headfirst into the floor, but he snags one of his strong arms around my waist and squeezes for emphasis. I can feel him smiling as he kisses the bare hip that is now jutting into the air.

"I've got you," he says.

With his free hand, he opens the door. Given that I'm now being carried ass-first into whatever is ahead, all I can see is the limestone floor of the maze-like passageway that we're leaving behind transition to the white marble of this new space. A thick layer of dark red bougainvillea vines shifts into place behind us, swallowing the door from view like a botanical curtain.

Flickering white candles of all sizes line the pathway, casting a soft, shifting glow behind us. In a few more steps, I hear the gentle rush of water. Hades finally comes to a stop and lowers me to my feet. The moment I have my balance, my gaze is drawn overhead.

Stars. No, not stars—*galaxies*. More than I've ever seen.

The night sky acts as the canopy of this large, enclosed courtyard. The entire space is ringed with tall columns that look especially white against the lush creeping vines, the blooms of which are the deepest, richest color I've ever seen. I'm wondering what variety they are, how they got them so dark, in the same way I'm considering the stars, and how they got them so bright, or the pool so serenely blue. Its inviting depth stretches long off to our right, with a waterfall on the far side, dropping off into nothingness. A thin layer of steam hangs over the water's surface.

It's overwhelming, almost intoxicating. It's as if every flower, every night sky, every body of water I've ever seen is layered on top of itself, hitting me all at once.

"It's like being in a painting," I murmur. "I've never seen so many constellations."

"I can give you one, if you like."

When my gaze returns to him, I notice that while I've been taking in our surroundings, my counterpart has only been taking in *me*.

I blush with an incredulous laugh. "You'll give me the stars?"

"I'll give you anything you want, little nymph."

With a smooth touch, he slips the pashmina from my shoulders and lets it drop soundlessly to the marble floor.

He works the buttons of his shirt, and it joins my wrap on the ground, along with his belt and shoes. I'm suddenly gawking at his body, wondering if I've ever seen such perfection. Smooth skin with undertones of warm honey. Wide shoulders and an equally strong torso. Muscles sculpted from marble, leading to a deep V that disappears into the top of his pants—which he is now hooking his thumbs into and sliding down, tugging off, stepping out of. His half-hard cock hangs heavy against his thigh. I drag my gaze up.

"I want you," I say softly.

He draws closer, until his forehead presses into mine. His hands come to my neck and the collar subtly tightens, followed by the sound of the buckle loosening. My limbs flood with panic.

He's taking it off.

"Wait." My hands gently curl over his. "I mean, sorry. *Sir*." His eyes glimmer with amusement at my attempt to redirect. "I'd like to keep it. I mean... Isn't this... How will people know I'm...?"

Yours?

His?

This adornment offers a certain level of comfort. Protection. Over the course of the evening so far, it has almost become my touchstone. My grounding point. He seems to see me weighing this.

"There are plenty of communal baths around the palace, but this one isn't open to the public. It's just us here. And you won't want to get this wet. The leather would get brittle. And your pretty neck needs to breathe."

In a few gentle movements, he slips the collar free, and though I've been naked this whole time, I suddenly feel it. He places it on the edge of a lounge chair, as if to show me that it's still there if I want it. Not a safe word, but perhaps a safety of sorts. The reassurance emboldens me.

I dip a toe into the water of the pool, sighing deeper before I can stop myself. "Oh, it feels perfect."

"The water in this bath comes from the same spring that feeds the river Styx," he says. "It's said to promise immortality."

I sink into its warm embrace, submerging myself to my collarbones and tipping my gaze to the sky. The water soothes every sore and over-sensitive spot on my body. My hair floats around me, and I gather it up with one hand, winding it into a knot that I tie at the base of my neck.

"Nobody really believes that stuff anymore, you know," I say with a sidelong glance.

Hades smirks as he slips into the pool behind me. "Nobody has to believe in death. It comes eventually, whether you believe it or not."

"Comforting," I deadpan.

"Would you rather I lie?"

I consider his question as I wade across the length of the pool to the infinity edge, where water drops hundreds of feet down the sheer rock face, disappearing into the hazy fog of the Styx. Beyond that are dark mountains, squares of farmland, and the sparkling lights of the city. I've never seen it from this vantage point. It looks like a faraway fairytale village, the kind you might find among someone's collection of hand-crafted miniatures, in which every shadowy structure is lit from within. A strange feeling stirs within me, like I'm standing outside my life looking in.

"It's different across the river," I say, almost to myself.

My quiet tone carries easily across the water, as does his reply.

"Different, maybe. But in many ways, the same. People will always find something to worship."

I know he's right. The old temples stand empty, relics of a time before everyone worshiped the almighty dollar or their own self-image. People tend to regard this realm in the agnostic sense. Maybe it exists, all these forces beyond our control, beyond the bubble of our social networks, our problems, our phones, but our interest is non-committal, inconsequential.

"Like my mom," I muse. "She maybe started as something good a long time ago – upholding all the old ways, being a champion of farmers, grocers – but over time she sold out to the same corporate greed as everyone else. All those farmers are now under contracts that mean they can barely keep afloat from season to season. They're practically indentured to the system. Farms that have been in their families for generations just..."

I realize I'm rambling, and I shake my head. "Sorry."

Before I can turn to find him, Hades is wading behind me, wrapping his arms around my torso, nuzzling the side of my bare neck.

"No need to apologize," he says. "You're passionate about this."

"I am. That's why I started the community gardens. They're under her company's umbrella, sure, but I like to think we're putting the power back in the hands of the people. Showing them they're... capable."

"You believe everyone has a green thumb?" he muses.

"I believe that if people continue to buy into the lie that one can only grow things by luck or favor or chance, we're always going to have imbalances in our system. Gardening, farming, cultivating—they want you to think you either have it or you don't, but in my experience it's a learned skill. Big Farma owns the majority of the market, but every little bit counts. The small things matter."

As he sways me in his arms, the water gently swishes with our movements. "I think you've got a delightfully defiant soul, and I like that about you."

"Really? I thought you liked me for my 'greedy, wet pussy.'"

He releases me, but I hear him smile. "Can't it be both?"

Across the courtyard, Nick-the-server has appeared through the hidden door and is leaving a tray at the edge of the pool. As we swim closer, he bows deeply.

"Sir. Lady. The service you requested."

Hades inclines his head graciously, as if he understands that the poor kid went from fangirling to possibly trying to overcompensate with seriousness.

"Thank you, Nicholas. See to our guests now, won't you?"

"As you wish, Your Darkness."

When the server disappears, Hades pulls me toward the edge, moving us slowly through the warm water.

"Your Darkness?" I tease.

"It's an old title. I have many. And I try not to get too hung up in the particulars."

I prop my elbows on the edge and smile as he plucks a strawberry off the tray and hovers it above my mouth. I wrap my lips around it and take a bite.

It feels intimate.

This moment. This courtyard. This private late-night spread, which is exactly what I need, especially since before heading for the ferry I was so racked with nerves that I didn't eat anything in the way of dinner.

I search through the multi-colored array of cheeses, meats, and fruits until I decide on a chunk of melon and pop it into my mouth. I hum at how sweet it is, how ripe, especially this late in the season. Hades watches me with adoration bordering on fascination. A small smile creeps across my lips.

"You're not how I thought you'd be," I admit.

"Oh?" he says. "Have you spent a lot of time thinking about how I'd be?"

I snag another snack from the tray. "I mean, who hasn't? You're *Hades.* The man, the myth, the meme."

There's genuine curiosity in his expression, and it gives his face a suddenly boyish quality.

"What's a meme?"

I almost choke on a bite of honeyed brie, and I cover my mouth with my forearm.

"Who doesn't know what a *meme* is? Have you been living under a rock?"

He shrugs, amused. "Of sorts."

Oh god. I'm not sure until this moment, but he's actually serious. And I find this so adorable that my smile comes bright and unbidden.

"A meme is an online image, basically, but the kind that becomes ubiquitous. And there's an image of you that made the rounds online a few years ago. You have to know the one. It was from that interview you did, with Hermes?"

"Hermes," he scoffs. "That sniveling gossip. Twists peo-ple's words without reason. But yes, to answer your ques-tion, I know the one."

"Well, regardless, people seem to think your resting face looks... disappointed. As in, 'let's attach this image of Hades looking disappointed to illustrate my exasperation with something, but in a humorous way.' That's what they call it. The Disappointed Hades."

He blinks. Then, his stony expression cracks open with a laugh.

"This is how you people are entertaining yourselves on the other side of the river? With my resting dick face? No wonder you aren't in a hurry to head home."

His laughter is contagious, and when he collapses against the edge of the pool in amusement, I find myself reveling in this rare moment of *him*. I snag his jaw, turning his broad smile toward me.

"I happen to like your resting dick face," I say. "But I like this more."

"Mm." He feigns nonchalance, but his smile simmers. "I like *you*."

I kiss him, and his mouth tastes sweet and sensual.

"So," I venture. "What happens from here?"

"What do you mean?"

I suck in a tentative breath. "I mean, how do these things usually go?"

He gives me a slow, assessing blink of his dark ocean eyes.

"Well. We eat. We bathe." I nod, as if those things are obvious. "And then we get some rest. Because—assuming you don't decide to escape during the night—you need to be prepared for your next day of training tomorrow."

A current of heat sparks to life under my skin when he says 'training.'

"So I can stay here?"

"As long as you like."

"I have my own room?"

"If you want. I have plenty of rooms. But I'd prefer you stay with me."

A long beat passes between us. The waterfall gurgles. The breeze rustles the hanging greenery. The current around us gently whirs.

I wonder why, of all the women in this sprawling palace, Hades himself has chosen me. Was our meeting by design or coincidence? I can't shake the feeling that he was waiting for me in that library, but how could that be possible? *Could it? Be possible?*

This whole night feels like a fever dream, and the only thing I'm sure of is that I want it to last. To immerse myself in it fully. To savor it until the very last moment. I don't want to spoil the perfect, shimmering illusion by asking questions whose answers don't really seem to matter.

"I'd prefer that, too," I say.

He nods once. It's decided, then.

I grab a triangle of crispy bread, a hunk of creamy cheese, and a thin slice of apple, sating my hunger as we settle into a comfortable silence. I try not to think about my phone, sitting somewhere in a lockbox, and all of the likely missed calls and messages. I haven't thought about it until this moment, actually, and the realization is a blend of liberating freedom and terrifying untetheredness.

"You're worried about what your family will think," he notes. It's not a question. "Your friends. Your mother."

"Yes."

He draws closer, tipping my head back until his lips graze mine. "Would you like me to help you forget?"

My eyes meet his, and the look twists through my center. I wet my lips.

"Yes."

In one smooth motion, he gathers me into his arms and wraps my legs around his waist, pressing my back against the edge of the pool. His mouth meets mine in a warm, possessive rush. I surrender to his lips with a moan. He kisses me like he's been starving for it. The little sounds

I make. This teasing of tongues, biting tug of teeth. This sure, intuitive *connection*.

I feel him getting hard, and I realize I don't know what the rules are now.

"You're still thinking," he murmurs. A small reprimand, brushing against my lips.

"Do I need permission?"

"Permission for what?"

"To touch you."

His eyes meet mine in a seductive, amused way that tugs through me, deep and low. It's only when his gaze dips to the place where my breasts are crowded against his chest that I realize how ridiculous my statement seems. My sex is snug against his firm lower abs. My hands have threaded into the wet hair along the back of his head.

"To touch me, or fuck me?"

My shuddering exhale falls across his mouth.

"Both."

His hands slide down to my waist and squeeze.

"Tell me how you want to get fucked."

"Hard," I breathe. "Now."

He lifts me onto the cool marble and hoists himself up after. Water cascades off of him as he climbs over me, kissing up the sensitive dip above my hip, biting the underside of my breast, licking a line up my exposed neck. His hand cradles the base of my head, angling it so he can claim my mouth with his, and my need for him returns with an aching urgency. I grip the thick length of him, guiding him against me, working him up and down my slit until he growls.

"Are you playing with me, princess? Or do you want my cock?"

"I want your cock," I breathe. "I want it so very much."

Though I asked for it, I don't expect it—the feel of him pressing inside me, stretching me beyond my limit, filling me up. I cry out against his mouth, digging my hands into his hair as pleasure and pain surge through me.

"You're sure?" he says. The force of his next thrust takes my breath, and I realize I have only taken him halfway. My pussy throbs around him with every frantic beat of my heart, both terrified and desperate to know if I can take any more.

"Yes," I whimper. I hold onto him so tightly my fingernails will probably leave half moons in his shoulders.

"Yes what?"

He sinks into me again, deeper than before. I gasp another desperate sound.

"Yes, sir. Please. Oh my god, it feels so good."

His muscles flex as he drags my thigh around his waist, angling himself so his next movement lands hard against my clit, at once gentle and fierce.

"This is why you came. You wanted to take my cock in your tight little cunt until I ruin you."

It's not a question. Still, I tip my head back, offering another gasping sigh.

"Yes," I beg. "Fucking ruin me."

"It'll be my pleasure."

His gaze goes hazy with lust as he buries himself again. And again. And again. Each time I scream louder, hold on tighter. His rhythm is fast and unrelenting and entirely fucking *perfect*, like he knows exactly how I want him, how I need him.

I almost never come like this. I'm not proud of how many times I've faked it. But there's nothing fake about this. The entire evening has felt like foreplay for this very moment, and he's so close to finishing me.

"Hades." I pant into his mouth. "I'm going to..."

"Yes," he says.

The sensation I've been chasing all night sucks me under, fast and all-consuming. He slows to deep, steady strokes as I fall apart.

"God," I moan. "Oh my god."

"Are you praying to me, princess?"

Maybe I am. My pussy pulses around him as I meet his movements, and I can't think when I'm still coming like this.

"Don't stop," I beg.

If it's possible, I feel him getting harder inside me, as if drawing out my pleasure is what gets him off. From the furrow between his dark brows, the fire in his smoldering eyes, I'm sure he's close.

"You haven't had enough yet?"

Sore. I'm so sore. But the thought of not having him inside me for a while longer—possibly forever—is complete insanity.

With a quick shift, I reverse our positions, rolling him underneath me. It's a calculated risk, but I'm rewarded when his head tips back with a groan. I angle my hips, testing the depth, finding a rhythm that leaves him sighing out curses toward the stars.

"Fuck. You move like you were made for me."

I nip his bottom lip with a teasing exhale. "You thought I was just a pretty face?"

The marble is cool under my knees, and I'm sure they'll be bruised tomorrow, but I don't care. I drive him home again, and again, with a quick, desperate pace that matches our panting breaths. He palms my ass, working me up and down on his cock.

"Not a chance. I mean, have you seen your tits?"

He sucks one of my sore nipples into his mouth for emphasis, and I laugh out a moan.

I love this. This give and take. It's easy. Insatiable. And I realize in my efforts to make him lose control, another orgasm is building within me. It's such a deep, impossible pleasure that holds me right at the edge. I grind harder against him.

"Should I..." I breathe. "Should you pull out?"

"If you want. But I can't father children, if that's what you're worried about. King of the Dead, and all."

I don't expect this, but in the moment, it hits me like a flash of relief. I also know every person who boarded the ferry had to submit a clean bill of health, same as me.

"So if I want you to fill me up with cum, you will?"

He grits his teeth, digging his fingers into my hip, wrestling with his own release. "Such a greedy girl. You want it already?"

"*You* want it already." My muscles burn, but I don't slow my pace. "You want to come so bad. I can feel it."

A low growl vibrates in his throat. "You'll be the death of me, Persephone."

"A thousand little deaths," I murmur.

"Even better."

He watches me ride him until his lust borders on agony. All at once, his resolve breaks. I can feel his cock throb inside me, so big and thick that the tide of my pleasure reaches its peak but won't quite crash.

The moment stretches, slow and seductive, like the soothing caresses of his lips, his tongue. My breath comes in a sharp gasp as he lifts me off of him. With sensual grace, he sits up and draws me against his chest, stroking his fingers along my slick center as I straddle his lap.

"Did you come again, princess?"

A blush creeps across my face. "Not yet, but I'm so—"

He swipes a stinging blow across my ass, and I yelp. I barely catch my breath before he lands another, and another.

"We don't leave things unfinished. You're going to stay here until you come for me."

I dig my knees into the smooth marble, simultaneously wanting to crawl away from him and inching my backend higher off his lap, begging for more, which he is happy to oblige. When the blows come faster, so do the building waves of pleasure.

"Does it feel good, little nymph? You like being punished like a very bad girl?"

I open my mouth to respond, but he smooths his hand between my legs and rubs me possessively. My breath breaks, and with it, so does everything holding back the pleasure that's been building.

The edge is sweet, and high, and I'm falling. Being pulled flush against him and rolled onto my back, with my legs spread wide and my body pulsing with aftershocks.

Hades bows between my thighs, nuzzling his face against my sex. "You taste so good after I fuck you."

My fingers grip into his hair with what little strength I have left.

"Oh, my... *Hades*."

He draws out my climax until I'm begging, and then he crawls over me, gathering me into his arms, hooking my thigh around him, kissing me deeply. He tastes sweet and salty, and my mind is so blissfully empty that I can't understand how I've ever existed anywhere but here.

We lie tangled together under the stars until the overwhelming ecstasy melts to a manageable buzz. Hades kisses my forehead, my temples, the tip of my nose. Then he scoops me up and eases us back into the warm, waiting water.

5

These are the desires I've harbored for years and never spoken aloud. The things I've been thinking about before I could possibly know such things exist, wondering with wide-eyed, heart-pounding intensity what happens to the princess after she's captured by the villain.

Being used.

Being punished.

Being worshiped by the god of a man that is leading me to his bed.

Everything about being here is pleasure like I've never imagined, and I mean this beyond the realm of physical touch. Every detail of this palace is designed to excite the senses. The way it smells warm like hints of bergamot and ginger and the woods at dusk, but only in glimpses, like trying to catch a shooting star. The way the colors are dark and vivid like a wet painting, and the food tastes like sin.

The way my steps softly patter along the cool floors as I walk barefoot toward his bedroom.

Hades's quarters open to a broad balcony with a stone balustrade that overlooks lands I've never seen, lying under a canopy of stars that looks as brilliant as it did in the bath. His bed is a sprawling stretch of luxury, with buttery soft linens and fluffy pillows you could almost melt into. Beside it, there's a backlit wall of toys. Dildos and vibrators. Paddles and whips. Bars with leather cuffs attached, as if he could decide at any moment to spread my legs wide and trap my wrists above my head.

He makes no mention of these things tonight, but the idea secretly thrills me as we climb into his bed, drunk on satisfaction, decadent food, and rich wine.

I can imagine my friend Psyche, who has been burned one too many times by the wrong kind of men and is now getting her PhD in clinical psychology, would tell me I'm suffering from Stockholm Syndrome at its finest. As my limbs grow heavy with sleep, I decide if it is... well... I'm content to be kept, held tight in this lust-drenched dream where I fall asleep in his arms.

Hades wakes me with the sunrise, enticing me with kisses and a warm cup of coffee. I sit upright in bed, attempting to sweep my sleep-mussed hair away from my face. It smells sweet and slightly floral, still damp from the late-night bath. I accept the beverage with murmured thanks. Hades stretches across the other side of the bed like a cat in the sun.

It wasn't a dream then. I'm actually in the palace across the river.

"I didn't think the sun would rise here," I admit.

"Apollo is an obstinate fuck," Hades shrugs. "It isn't worth the effort to try and stop him. And I happen to like the way it makes everything look. Warm. Alive."

A small smile plays at the edge of my lips. "The King of the Dead prefers things that look alive? The irony."

"Death has no meaning without life. Nor life without death, some would argue."

"No pleasure without pain," I add.

His eyes glint. "Hmm. Wise *and* beautiful."

Our kisses deepen. He drags me against him, and the blankets are already slipping away from my shoulders. He winds my long hair around his fist, smiling as my mouth opens with the faintest gasp. I'm in the middle of teasing his tongue with mine when I hear, "What in the fresh hell is this?"

I spring away from Hades with a start, only to find that the words came from the woman standing across the room, looking unfazed by our bemusement.

I grasp at the blankets and cover myself, while Hades draws himself upright, making no effort to do the same.

"Juno. What did I tell you about barging in like this?"

He says it in a chastising groan, the way one might to an impetuous child. But this woman isn't a child. She's all voluptuous curves and brown sugar skin, with a mane of dark curls that bounces as she sashays about the room in her fitted sleeveless blouse, chino pants, and the kind of heels that ooze confidence. I feel the color drain from my face as panic settles into my belly.

What if she's his girlfriend? His *wife*?

"You've been ignoring my messages all morning," she continues, snagging a pastry off the breakfast tray and waving it our general direction accusingly. "I wish you'd accept calls like the rest of the world. Your current system leaves a bit to be desired."

She tosses the remainder of the pastry toward the rail of the balcony, narrowly missing a trio of crows. Their wings flutter with a loud chorus of caws as they shift to miss the toss. She scowls when they settle back onto the balcony as if to mock her.

Hades presses his mouth into a line of annoyed amusement. "I've been a bit *preoccupied*."

"I can see that." She sinks across a lounge chair near the open balcony doors with a dramatic sigh. "At least *somebody's* getting laid around here, I suppose."

"Hades," I murmur. "Should I...?"

He gives me a reassuring shake of his head.

"Juno, this is Persephone. Persephone, Juno. She's a life-long friend. Also happens to be married to my brother."

"*Fraternity* brother," Juno clarifies. "And I'll have you recall that I'm in the group, too, whether I'm married to that asshole or not. Don't act as if I'm an accessory to your silly little boys' club. I was sworn in, same as the rest of you."

He breathes a long sigh from his nose as if they've had this conversation a time or two as well. "Can we argue about this some other time? We were in the middle of something."

She wipes the flaky pastry crumbs from her fingers. "Nonsense. Join me for breakfast. I'm too angry to be alone, and I want to learn more about your friend. Persephone, was it? Where have I heard that name before?"

Fuck.

Another wave of panic rushes in to replace the one that recently receded, joined by a new set of questions. What if she knows me? My friends? My colleagues? My mother?

"She runs a company across the river," Hades says as he pulls a sarong from the dresser and secures it around his waist. I'm grateful when he tosses me one as well.

"An entrepreneur," Juno notes, intrigued. "Which company?"

I pause, knotting the fabric at my bosom, the way one wears a towel after a shower. "It's just a community garden project. It's called Bounty."

My voice goes up at the end like a question. Bounty is a modest success, but it's not a household name. I'm hoping she falls into the camp of those who have never heard of it.

Her eyes alight with interest. "You're Demeter's daughter?"

Busted.

The way my gaze drops to the trays of food on the table in front of us answers this question for her. She gives a low hum of satisfaction before snagging a bunch of grapes and popping one into her mouth.

"This just got interesting," she laughs. She calls to Hades across the room. "Did you seriously steal Demeter's daughter?"

Hades comes up behind me, giving my shoulders a reassuring massage. "I did not *steal* her. She was invited. You know the rules."

"You've done some pretty ridiculous shit in your time," Juno continues, "but this might top it all."

He waves her off before sinking into the chair beside mine and pouring us a pair of sparkling breakfast cocktails. My hands are trembling as I accept the delicate flute. I force myself to take a sip, hoping the fizzy-sweet goodness will distract from my mental spiral.

I attempt to sound innocent and uninterested as I ask, "How do you know my mother?"

"Everyone knows your mother. She's made sure of it," Juno says. "Powerful people like to surround themselves with other powerful people. And Big Farma has lined a lot of pockets. Completely cornered the agricultural market, as I'm sure you're aware. There's not a single crop within a thousand miles that isn't their intellectual property, right down to the seeds, and those farmers are left groveling at her almighty feet every season, begging for her favor. It'd be impressive if it weren't so damn corrupt."

I've heard these criticisms of my mother's enterprise my entire life. At times, I've been inclined to share them, albeit secretly. But I like to think she isn't all bad. She's funding my project, after all. She's approved every request I have for expansion. But still, my operation is small potatoes compared to hers – quite literally. I'm pretty sure the seeds she allows us to use were in fact genetically modified to produce smaller yields, though I don't have any proof of this.

"Everyone has to eat," I offer. It's the same line I've fed to reporters for years when presented with hard-hitting questions or opinions.

Juno returns my smile.

"Yes, but some of us eat better than others." She pops another grape in her mouth for emphasis.

Hades reaches under the table and slides a comforting hand along my thigh. It settles my nerves a bit, knowing that he's seemingly on my side. It's an odd paradox: the villain, the protector.

"More to the matter at hand," he says. "What did Zefs do this time?"

Juno's pleasant demeanor melts into a growl. "He fucked that vicious bitch from Sparta."

Hades squints, thinking. "Helen?"

"Leda!" She spits the name like it's fire. "He's always been a philanderer, but I swear to you, Hades, this time I'll have his balls. I'm done."

"You said this last time."

"And if I had followed through with my threats of castration, we wouldn't be here now, would we? Do you know she had the nerve to say she didn't *know* she was sleeping with my husband? As if anyone doesn't know

Zefs on sight, with his long stupid flowing hair and that ridiculous thunderbolt tattoo he's so proud of." Juno pours herself a cocktail and downs it with a tip of her head. "Her excuse was that she was under the influence of psychedelic drugs and thought he was a swan. Who the hell fucks a swan? Even the people hanging around here at your depraved parties aren't fucking swans."

I realize Hades is barely containing his smirk. When he catches my gaze, he raises a playful eyebrow at me, and suddenly I'm barely containing mine as well.

"Perhaps you could use a little depravity yourself, then," Hades offers. "Maybe hang around here for a bit and cool off. You know there's always a room for you."

When Juno grabs a large knife from the butcher block, I'm suddenly concerned she's about to meet our quiet amusement with imminent violence. But in the end, she simply snags a bright pomegranate from the nearby bowl of fruit and slices it in half with a loud *chop*.

"You know I don't like to hang around here too long. It always gives the feeling that death is clinging to me," she shudders. To me she adds, "Speaking of which, you'll need this."

She grabs a wooden spoon and gives the fruit a few firm smacks until the seeds fall out. The sight brings to mind Hades's hands on me, and despite the ache in my backside, I think I wouldn't mind him smacking me with that wooden spoon. When he catches me watching like he knows this is exactly what I'm thinking, I blush.

"You'll need to eat three of these, each day you're here," Juno says, collecting a trio of tendrils from the cutting board and adding them to the plate of assorted sweet and savory pastries in front of me.

Hades elaborates. "This is how you can stay in my world without being claimed by death."

"Immortality?"

"In a sense."

"'In a sense,'" Juno mocks. "Why are you always trying to be so mysterious? Yes, to answer your question, sweetheart. Immortality. If you want to continue to enjoy all the forbidden fruits on this side of the river, you'll need it."

I consider this before slipping one of the juicy seeds into my mouth. I take them one after another, like aspirin the morning after too much booze. Juno sprinkles hers on the top of a slice of toast coated with whipped cream cheese before taking a big bite.

"So, you'll stay," Hades prompts her. "Let this blow over."

"Just for today. I can't leave Ares unchaperoned all weekend. You know teenage boys and their raging hormones. If he's left alone too long, he's bound to start

World War IV. And somehow, it'll be my mess to clean up. It's not like Zefs ever lifts a finger to help." She groans, working herself into a rage. "Why did I marry him again?"

"Love," Hades says simply. "And good hair. But mostly love, I think."

She sighs at the memory. "God, that gorgeous hair. I've got half a mind to shave it off in his sleep."

"Do you want me to talk to him?"

"No. Yes. Maybe," she says. "But don't placate him. You know it goes straight to his head."

Hades gives her a patient nod. "I know."

As he rises from the chair, I'm inclined to do the same, but he lowers me back into my seat with a kiss on the top of my head.

"You should stay and finish eating," he says. "You'll need your strength for what's to come later."

I catch his gaze. "What is to come later?"

"We're attending the party in the main pavilion, with you as my guest."

I both know and don't know what this entails. My attention flits to the collar waiting on the table beside the bed, and my pulse ticks with excitement and trepidation.

"Am I ready for that?"

His smile is wicked. "You will be. Juno can help you get dressed."

At this, her simmering annoyance morphs into enthusiasm.

"Yes! I love playing dress-up." Her large brown eyes dance over my details, assessing. "What look are we going for here? Innocent victim? Secret sexpot?"

"Willing captive," he says, throwing me a wink.

When he leaves us alone, I swell with a steadying breath.

"So," I say to Juno. "What do you do?"

Without a hint of irony she replies, "I'm a marriage counselor."

Finished with her meal—or perhaps this conversation—she draws herself up from the table and crosses to one of the closets, swinging open the double doors with a flourish and sifting through her options. She begins tossing possibilities onto the nearby ottoman.

I wonder about the origin of this closet of clothes. Wonder how many women Hades has brought into his bed, enticed into this type of arrangement. I suddenly don't have much of an appetite, opting instead for pouring myself another glass of boozy bubbles.

"Do you do this a lot?" I offer, tentatively joining Juno across the room, where she is puzzling over a pair of heels. "Dress Hades's girls for his parties?"

She scrunches her nose, tossing me a quizzical look over her shoulder. "Hades doesn't have girls."

I blink at this. "Never?"

"I mean, not *never*," she says. "Just not usually."

I wet my lips. "Or... men, perhaps?"

She pauses now, dropping the dress she's been holding so that she can study me. I'm not sure what she's looking for in my expression, but she seemingly finds it, nodding to herself as she continues her raid.

"Hades is very particular in his interests. Not many women meet his standards."

I'm trying to put my finger on this feeling buzzing in my body. Disbelief? Possibly... delight? I want to know what standards he has exactly, and how I do or don't live up to them, though I know she isn't the one to ask.

"Why does he host these parties, then?" I press.

She cackles at my innocence.

"For the *life* of it, of course." At my obvious confusion, she adds, "The dead always covet the living. And there's nothing like the energy of a party—the absolute shared *pleasure* of it—to make one feel alive. Don't you agree?"

"But Hades isn't... dead." I feel ridiculous saying it out loud. Juno doesn't give it a second thought.

"Hades is Hades," she says, waving a hand.

She spins toward me now, taking a moment to twist pieces of my hair around her fingers and to loosen the knot of my sarong, allowing it to slip to the floor. I'm alarmed by the sudden closeness—by my sudden nakedness—and for a second, I wonder where the collar is. Do I need it now, to protect me from Juno? I find myself calculating how quickly I could sprint across the room and grab it.

"I feel like you're a Spring," she murmurs, half to herself. "But…"

When she taps a finger against her lips, I realize that she has undressed me the way one does a favorite doll. Her determined gaze travels down my body before sliding back up. In an instant, she's digging through the clothing options again.

"How do you feel about bondage?"

6

When I step out of the dressing room, Hades does a double-take. The book he's reading finds its way to an end table. He has to readjust himself in his pants before he's able to draw himself fully upright. As he opens his mouth to form words, they never seem to come.

I give him a coy shrug, as if to ask, *Do you like it?*

He drags his knuckles across his smile in a gesture that says, *Oh, I more than like it.*

"Doesn't she look gorgeous?" Juno declares, emerging from the bathroom behind me. "Hell, I'd fuck her."

With Juno's help, I decided on a black leather body harness, complete with garters and cuffs around my thighs. They're visible beneath the short, pleated black skirt, like the strappy triangles hugging the curves of my breasts are peeking from the V of my button-down top, which is tied at my waist. When paired with Juno's hair and make-up magic—all dramatic eyes, pouty bee-stung lips, and my hair falling over my shoulders in innocent strawberry waves—the effect is intoxicating. I look every bit the virginal vixen. And I feel sexy as hell.

Hades prowls toward me as Juno collapses onto the sofa, as if a morning of playing dress-up has left her entirely spent. He runs his fingers along the collar, which I fastened around my neck as a finishing touch. When he gives me another slow once over, my skin comes alive under his probing gaze.

"Yes," he murmurs. "This will do nicely."

As an afterthought, he crosses to the wall of toys and retrieves a shimmery, gold chain that sparkles under the backlight. I don't realize until he clips it to my collar that it's a leash. I'm hyper-aware of the gentle pressure at my throat as he gives it a tug. Arousal spreads through me, followed by goosebumps.

"Are you ready to be deflowered, little nymph?"

A surprised chortle escapes me. "I think you're a bit late for that."

"No, I'm not. Because no one before me matters. And you've never been fucked like this." His voice has an edge that draws my gaze to his and holds it there. "Spread open wide in front of a room full of people. Teased beyond your breaking point. Begging for your own release."

An electric current of anticipation runs through me. I realize I'm biting into my lower lip. When my mouth parts, now it's I who is not sure what to say.

"The terms of our agreement still stand. If at any point you prefer to leave…" He shrugs as if it's that simple.

I venture a glance at Juno, who is now preoccupied with scrolling through her phone.

"Is she coming with us?" I ask.

I'd swear she isn't paying attention until she waves a hand over her head, never lifting her gaze.

"You two go ahead without me. I'll catch up with you later. Maybe grab dinner with me, before I head home? Assuming you're done with your sexcapades by then."

Hades chuckles, lowering his voice. "Are you scared to be alone with me, princess?"

"Of course not," I say. "But this time, we won't be alone, will we?"

He meets my doe eyes with a subtle shake of his head.

"No. We won't."

The idea both thrills and terrifies me. I feel the straps of the body harness tighten against my skin as I swell with a breath. I think of what Hades said to me the previous evening in the library.

You'll become mine to use as I please.

If I want to fuck you, I'll fuck you.

If I want to share you, I'll share you.

I can pleasure you or deny you or discipline you.

You'll give me whatever I want, without hesitation. And in exchange I'll give you what you want. Things you don't even know you want.

I'll worship your greedy little cunt like a goddess.

And I won't stop until I've pushed you past the edge of absolute oblivion.

The memory of it tingles across my skin like a threat and laces my veins like a sweet, aching promise.

"Well then," I say. "Lead the way."

The seductive glow of the burning lamps and candles that line the hall shifts across us as we make our way through the private passage. As the thrumming bassline of the music grows louder, so does the pounding of my pulse.

I know we're getting closer.

In this part of the palace, it doesn't matter if it's dawn or midnight. There are no windows, and time ceases to exist. The moment we step through the last set of doors, I'm not naked, but I might as well be.

We've referred to the main space where the parties happen as many things. A ballroom. A pavilion. But honestly, this is an atrium, with higher levels open to the center, able to view the entire scene. Large columns in the grand, Greco-Roman style stretch stories high, but the furnishings remind me of vintage Vegas. Everything is low and loungey: exuding opulence, teeming with activity, primed for sin.

I'm more confident than I was the first time I set foot in this room, and as such, I catch more of the details. I collect them greedily, as if each one is a rare gem I could slip into my pocket.

The tufted runner that my heels sink into as we make our way into the room, that feels like walking across a pathway of fresh moss.

The terraced pits sunken into the main floor, littered with vibrant pillows and inviting casual orgies.

The beautiful cages suspended from the ceiling, with actual people inside: some dancing, some masturbating, others begging for release.

The large curved bar made of dark marble, with backlit bottles and mirrors behind it, where people laugh and chat over their libations like this is any typical party.

But, obviously, this isn't a typical party.

The shushing sound of murmurs follows us as we wind further down the pathway, like silk sliding across skin. A hush ripples in our wake. So many eyes are on us, and the instinct to cover myself is so profound that I clasp my fingers around the hem of my skirt, as if I could suddenly make it long enough to hide the cheeky glimpse of my ass.

"You're beautiful," Hades murmurs against my ear. "Let them see you. Let them *want* you."

His words send chills down my neck, teasing my nipples into taut points. When I let my tentative gaze drift around us, I see clearly that they do want me. It's in the hungry glint of their eyes, the way white teeth sink into full lips, how their hands absently caress their own skin. To accept the attention—to *welcome* it—after I've spent much of my life practicing the subtle art of pushing it away, hits me like a sudden rush.

How long have I been hiding?

My chest swells with a breath, heightening my awareness of the fact that everyone can see it.

That I'm braless.

That I'm horny.

That I'm *human*.

Hades grazes a thumb across the thin fabric of my top, drawing me back to him. I meet his gaze like a lifeline, and he holds it steady for a few reassuring beats.

"How does it feel?" he asks.

"It feels..." My tongue slides between my lips, like I can taste the words, the sensation. "Like a kind of freedom."

His eyes flicker with a smile. "Funny, isn't it? That being tied up makes you feel free?"

I breathe out a laugh, and it melts some of the residual tension.

With a gentle tug of the leash, he leads me off the carpeted pathway and into the crowd. It parts before us as if by magic. Even the people in various states of undress, some of whom never stop fucking and sucking each other as we pass, take notice, as if our very presence is heightening their pleasure.

Hades makes small talk with many as he passes. Some I can tell he doesn't know, but others seem like regular acquaintances, maybe even old friends, the last of which is, "Ty, a pleasure."

Ty is a man of imposing stature, but even his commanding size doesn't detract from the fact that he's accompanied by three people on leashes, all presumably submissives like me, and all incomprehensibly beautiful.

Two are women and the other is a man, though he's wearing a cage over his cock that gives me a strange reassurance that he probably couldn't use it without permission. He has a lithe frame, boyish hair, and pouty, almost feminine lips. The taller woman has an hourglass figure and reminds me of a dark Jessica Rabbit, all swaying hips and seductive curves. The shorter one has cute, petite breasts and spunky brown pigtails sprigging from atop her head.

They eye me curiously, one of them twisting her leash around her finger, another bouncing on the balls of her feet with the energy of an excited lapdog.

"Can we?" the smaller woman begs. "Can we play with her, please?"

"We love a new friend," the curvier woman says.

The guy tongues the corner of his lips. "We'll be very gentle."

"Cerberus, quiet!" The man yanks the leash to calm the enthusiastic begging and bouncing, but they still eye me excitedly. "Sorry. They haven't been walked in a while."

He grins now, giving me a once over. "Tell me, Hades, does your little pet play well with others?"

"Mm, Persephone? She hasn't been socialized much," Hades replies, cutting me an amused sideways glance. "But she's a fast learner."

"Cerberus," Ty says again. This time, they all turn their heads to him in unison, as if this is a collective name. "This is Persephone."

I don't realize I've stepped closer to Hades until he circles an arm around my waist. He strokes the bare skin of my midriff reassuringly and presses his lips to my temple.

"They just want to play, princess. Can you be a good girl and let them get acquainted?"

I swallow the knot in my throat. I have no idea what I'm agreeing to, but I hear myself saying, "Yes, sir."

He uses the leash to draw me closer to the pack. The trio is eager. They're suddenly so close that I'm engulfed in the smell of them: something sweet and familiar, like vanilla ice cream on a hot summer day. The guy with the cock cage and the boy-band features trails a tentative touch up my lower belly, like he's wiping off a melty line of it that has dripped down my skin.

"Hi, Persephone," he says. "I'm Yesterday."

The taller woman has drawn in close on my other side. I can hear the smile in her deep sigh as she nuzzles her nose against my neck. Her voice is as seductive as she is.

"I'm Tomorrow."

The other drops to her knees in front of me and traces a finger along one of the cuffs around my thigh, stroking back and forth, all impish and eager.

"I'm Today."

"We're Cerberus," they say in unison.

I don't know what to make of this, and I find myself standing stock still as Tomorrow's nuzzling turns into gentle kisses, which she nips along the sensitive space between my neck and shoulder. On my other side, Yesterday gently strokes my waist and fingers the knotted front of my shirt. Today runs her tongue up my inner thigh in tentative little strokes.

This should feel weird. Three people I don't know, half-naked, with their hands on me, while Hades and his friend watch, commenting on how good we're being and how well we're getting along. But it's actually... *really* fucking hot.

Yesterday loosens the knot of my shirt.

"Can we take this off?"

I open my mouth to protest when Tomorrow's hands slide up to frame my face, gently threading her fingers into my hair. She kisses me in a way that begs complete surrender. I feel my lips part, feel her tongue tease mine. I've never kissed a woman before, and I'm surprised by how feminine she feels, and by how much that turns me on. When she pulls away, her gaze dances across mine.

"I think we can take it off," she tells him with a smirk.

Suddenly they're helping each other slide the shirt off my shoulders and dropping it to the floor.

"There's no need to hide such gorgeous tits," she purrs.

Meanwhile, Today has trailed her caressing touches under my skirt, along the curve of my ass, up to the waistband of my strappy thong.

"This, too?" she coos, already tugging the underwear down over my hips.

My breath comes quicker with the rush of my own arousal. I can feel the flush creeping up my neck, the wetness gathering between my thighs.

"I don't think I—"

"You're not here to think," Tomorrow says, stroking my cheek again and drawing me into another deep kiss. "You're here to feel. Does it feel good?"

Yesterday draws a line down my breasts until he reaches the peak of my nipple. When he circles it with his finger, a soft moan escapes me.

"Oh, she likes that," he says to Tomorrow.

Embarrassment burns hot across my face as my obvious excitement grows. Today is still on her knees in front of me, and without my panties in her way, she reaches up and strokes my sex.

I yelp in surprise, snapping my knees together and causing her to giggle. Ty gives her leash a reprimanding tug.

"Cerberus," he warns in a low voice. "Behave."

"Yes, sir," they chant, all sing-songy and seductive.

"Today didn't mean to upset you," Yesterday says. His lazy circles turn into tentative flicks of my nipple, up and down.

Tomorrow smooths her hands down my neck, caressing my other breast.

"She just gets…" She pauses, licking the sensitive bud while her counterpart continues to tease the other. "Excited."

What the fuck is happening?

I put a hand on each of their shoulders to steady myself. Tomorrow guides the touch down, cupping it over one of her full breasts. Up until now, I realize my hands have been uselessly hanging by my sides. Now, they have developed a mind of their own, exploring warm skin and firm muscles. I'm somehow surprised by how good it feels to touch them. Almost as good as being touched.

"That's it," Yesterday coaxes.

When he moves his mouth to my breast, matching the flicks of Tomorrow's tongue, I find myself with my fingers threaded into their hair. The sensation of them teasing me at the same time is so good that even when I open my eyes and realize we've got a small audience, I don't care.

Hades's sidelong stare is approving and hungry.

No hiding, it seems to say. Not from all the eyes watching me. Not from this pleasure.

Today is massaging my thighs again, and this time I spread them wider, giving her unspoken permission to explore. She does. Her delicate fingers spread wetness between my lips, over my clit, dipping inside me with tentative strokes. She adds a second, then a third, laughing as she attempts to fill me up.

"Mmm, she's so wet," Today sighs. She withdraws her fingers with a satisfied grin, sucking them into her mouth.

Tomorrow returns to my mouth, kissing me again. "Do you want more?"

The words come out before I can think them.

"Yes. Please."

She guides my mouth to her neck, and I'm kissing her, nibbling down her chest. I find myself tugging her hard nipple between my teeth, greedy for the velvet sighs she's making.

"Ooh, she bites," Tomorrow laughs, dragging my mouth back up to hers.

"Is that what you like, pet?" Yesterday asks, pinching my breasts as his tongue interrupts the kiss and takes over. "You want us to eat you up?"

They return their rapt attention to my pleasure, and suddenly I'm being eased into the embrace of a nearby sofa. Like everything else, I'm not entirely sure how this happens. One moment I'm on my feet, and the next I'm spread wide with Today kneeling between my legs, rubbing her face against my pussy. I moan, surprised by the way my hips roll against her mouth as she licks me. I feel her hum in satisfaction as Tomorrow and Yesterday tuck themselves onto either side of me. Without the added effort of standing, I'm lost to sensation.

Today licks.

Tomorrow caresses.

Yesterday tugs.

They stroke my nipples, and my clit, and I'm close to tumbling over the edge. The twitch of my nerve endings every time they tease me in tandem, it's all too much. But I also realize with acute panic that I'm not supposed to come—at least not without permission.

I attempt to draw myself out of the haze, gazing down the tether that connects me to the master of my pleasure. I wrap a hand around it and give an urgent tug.

"Hades," I pant. "Sir. Can I come please?"

"Sorry, what was that?" Hades says sweetly, as if he hadn't heard. He has drawn close enough to sweep a loose lock of hair from my face.

"Please." I shift my hips against the eager motion of Today's mouth. "I'm so close."

"Oh? You're close?"

I slip closer to ecstasy, urging myself there while Hades watches.

"Yes," I pant. "I'm right—"

There. I'm *right* there. At least, I am, until Hades flashes Ty a devious smile.

"Sorry, friend. I think she's had enough."

"Enough," Ty says.

With a single yank, he tugs Cerberus toward him. They take a collective stumbling step back. My tits pop out of their mouths, leaving my nipples hard and glistening with their saliva. My throbbing pussy is suddenly aching with the absence of touch. I don't realize I expected Hades to encourage my climax until I see them being dragged away at his word.

I writhe against nothing, at once ashamed and irritated and wanting.

"No. Wait. *Please*," I breathe.

When my hand reaches to meet my need, Hades tightens his hold on my leash, pinching the collar at my neck enough to elicit a whimper. I grip it with both hands to keep from choking. My eyes meet his, wide and desperate.

"You've had enough fun for now," he says. "And if you touch yourself like that again without my permission, I won't let you come for a fucking month."

My pulse flutters in my throat. I swallow hard.

"Yes. Sir."

Hades's counterpart laughs, leading the trio back to him with little sugar cubes as treats. They open their mouths and stick out their tongues, and he places one on each, murmuring praise. I have a feeling there's more than simple sweetness in those treats, but even so, I'm suddenly envious.

"It was good catching up with you, Hades," the man says. "Perhaps we'll run into each other a bit later?"

"Perhaps," Hades replies, inclining his head.

"This was fun," Yesterday offers.

"Next time," Tomorrow winks.

"Bye for now," Today teases with a wave, scrunching her cute little nose, still wet from burying her face between my legs.

I watch them turn, and suddenly, I'm on my feet.

I'm grateful to still be wearing my skirt when Hades leads me away, though it's short enough to barely constitute as a garment. My tits are on full display, and if not for the skirt, my pussy and ass would be too. I'm hyper aware of the collar as I attempt to swallow the heady combination of desire and disappointment.

"Did I do something wrong, sir?" I ask, keeping close to Hades's side as he saunters through the room.

"Not at all," he replies easily.

"Then why did you pull me away?"

"Because I'm not ready for you to come yet."

I know I sound like a petulant child when I say, "But why?"

He stops abruptly, spinning to give me a warning look and tucking a finger under my chin so I catch every moment of it.

"Because I love the way you look when you're desperate and horny. And because when I fuck you up there on that altar, I want you to beg for my cock like you've never begged before."

My gaze follows his to the sprawling marble altar at the back of the room, raised like a stage, with a statue of him sitting on a throne, holding court. Small offerings are scattered around his large stone feet.

The altar of Hades.

The Hades standing before me slowly traces one of the triangle straps outlining my breasts, bringing my attention back to him.

"And because you love it. Don't you—" He sweeps his thumb across my nipple until my eyes roll shut with pleasure. "—love it?"

His touch slips away just as quickly as he offered it. I run my tongue between my lips and sigh out a shaky exhale.

"I do."

His mouth twitches with a glimmer of a smile.

"I thought you might." He begins sauntering toward the bar, leading me by the shimmery chain that links us. "Let's get a drink, shall we?"

7

The bar in the center of the atrium is a flurry of activity, but we don't have to wait to be served. Guests in clothing that ranges from full evening wear to absolutely nothing, and all levels of undress in between, are eager to give up their seats. Hades attempts to deter their departures with an affable raise of his hand, but it's no use. An entire eight-seat section of the bar opens up as the guests clear a path for us, excited to have the chance to speak with the host up close. I half-expect them to ask him to sign autographs, and I wonder if he ever has. I can imagine women passing him Sharpies and jutting out their chests, eager to be marked by him.

When they drift away, a welcome sense of privacy settles over us. We're positioned at the apex of the curved bar, which is the perfect spot to see and be seen, but for the first time this evening, it's as if everyone has reverently averted their stares. Or at least if they haven't, they're being more discreet about it.

Hades orders us a couple of glasses of wine, drawing me against him while we wait.

"You're so famous," I tease.

He scoffs in modest response.

I laugh. "There's literally a marble statue of you in this room."

"Are you sure it's me? I've always thought it wasn't a very good likeness."

I lean into his embrace, bringing my smile close to his. "I tend to agree you're sexier in person."

The server appears beside us, producing two crystal glasses and filling them with pours of the deepest red. Hades swirls the wine before taking a swig.

"I tend to think," he says, passing me a glass, "that this will taste better on your lips."

He watches me take a slow sip—dark and smooth, with a fruity finish—before drawing me into a sensual kiss.

"What you were saying earlier," I murmur against his mouth, "about fucking me on the altar. Did you mean that?"

"Every word."

I straddle his thigh as I press myself closer, kissing deeper. "It sounds hot."

"Mmm. And you wouldn't happen to be trying to get yourself off against my thigh right now, would you?"

I attempt—rather unsuccessfully—to still my undulating movements, while nibbling his bottom lip. My body seems determined to finish what was started with Cerberus.

"Of course not."

He laughs. "You're lucky you're a delightful companion, because you're a terrible liar."

I thread my fingers into his hair, noticing how his mouth feels so different from Tomorrow's when she caressed me with her full feminine lips, and even from the pleasure of Yesterday's searching tongue. It's a welcome difference, unique only to the two of us, and I revel in it.

Hades's hands are roving up the backs of my thighs, beneath my skirt, kneading my ass. We carry on like this for a few luscious minutes, but we're interrupted when I hear, "Speak of the devil. How've you been, H?"

Hades and I both glance over at the wiry woman with caramel skin and glossy black hair, cut blunt with straight bangs. She wears a shimmery gold top and a belly chain above her dark pants, and she's at least a head shorter than me. She looks exotic. Glamorous. And with the haughty way she's eyeing us, I hate her immediately.

"Hello, Theo," Hades says coolly. "I thought you were back across the river."

She shrugs. "I traded a thing for a thing. Wound up with one of your silly gold coins. Found myself here. Funny how that happens, isn't it?"

"Hilarious," he offers without humor.

She gives me an unimpressed once-over. "Who's this?"

"She's not your concern."

Theo exhales a bitter laugh. "I see. Not even important enough to name. For a moment you had me worried."

Hades's eyes narrow. "You should be worried, if you keep saying things like that."

I recognize his warning tone, but if Theo does as well, she doesn't heed it. I bristle as she draws closer.

"Oh. You don't want her to know?" she continues. "That she'll never be anything more than your new toy."

Suddenly, she grabs the chain connected to my neck and yanks. I give a choking cough of surprise as I nearly topple off of Hades's lap. With predatory speed, he sweeps me to my feet, pulling himself upright and tucking me halfway behind him with a single strong arm, hackles raised.

"*You* might have been a toy, Theo. *She* is a queen. Touch her again and you'll find out exactly how insignificant you are."

At this, the whites of Theo's teeth flash. With a growl, she lunges at Hades like a crazed housecat, but he deflects her attack with the grace of a panther. He holds her wrists so tightly I'm surprised they don't snap. She is laughing as she struggles against his touch.

"Oh, H. You know I like it rough."

"Settle down, or I'll have you deported."

She glances over his shoulder at me, curling her nose the way one might at roadkill.

"What do you see in her anyway? So pale she almost looks dead already."

Hades snarls. "You insult her again, and I'll ban you from crossing the river even after your dying breath. I'll leave your filthy soul to wander the earth for eternity."

"I'm just telling you what no one else will have the balls to," she hisses. "She looks exactly the same as every other lily-white daddy's money bitch from across the river. And I'll bet she's a lousy fuck, too."

At this, Theo manages to slip one of her thin wrists from Hades's grasp. She grabs a lowball glass from the bar and smashes it across the side of his head. The glass shatters. Blood probably splatters, too. I'm not sure, because all I know is that I'm suddenly lunging forward, wrapping the chain of my leash around Theo's neck.

Strength I didn't know I possess vibrates through me. I twist until her back is tight against my front as she flails, gurgling choking noises. I maybe see Hades touch a hand to his head, see it come away crimson, but I'm not sure.

All I know for sure is that this bitch is going *down*.

She attempts to stomp my feet, claw my forearms, and buck her head into my chest. I snug the leash tighter and pull hard, knocking her off balance and dragging her behind me until she's clawing at her neck.

For a few horrifying heartbeats, I realize I'm not going to stop.

It's only when I hear the bewildered shouts of the guards who are rushing toward us that I release her. The shimmery chain slithers to the ground. She writhes, choking and gasping, on the floor.

"Are you okay?" I hear the guards saying. "My lady, are you okay?"

I realize belatedly that they're not asking her. They're asking *me*.

I stammer. I don't know how to answer their questions, and I don't have the brain power to form a response.

By the time they're cuffing her, the scene is playing out in slow motion, and my adrenaline is bottoming out. Our veil of privacy lifted some time ago, and we're now surrounded by gaping onlookers. I stare down at the woman's tear-streaked scowl and the angry red welts on her neck, wondering what the fuck came over me.

What have I done?

I've never even been in a bar fight. I've certainly never choked someone with a leash for insulting me and my… whatever Hades is to me. My vision blurs with the threat of tears. I sway on uneasy legs, and Hades catches me.

"Persephone!"

"I'm sorry," I choke. "I'm so sorry. I was—"

"It's okay." He tucks me against his chest. "Are you okay?"

"Yes," I nod. Followed quickly by, "No. I dunno. I didn't mean to hurt her. I'm not sure—"

"It's okay," he insists.

I realize he's holding a wad of bar napkins to his temple.

"Fuck. Are *you* okay?" I manage.

He attempts to wave me off, but I turn his head to get a better look at the wound. It's not quite as bad as I expected, given the amount of blood, but it stands to reason that head wounds—like fingers or toes—tend to bleed more than makes sense.

"Sir," one of the guards says, appearing at his side. "I've called for the doctor. You need medical attention."

Hades sighs, pulling the napkins away again to inspect.

"I think I just need to sit down."

The guard clears a path through the spectators and guides us to a semi-circular sofa. The patrons who are occupying it quickly disperse, and Hades sinks onto it, tucking me across his lap. A server brings him a fresh drink. This time it's the sweet, spicy liquor that we enjoyed in the library, since perhaps this situation calls for something stronger than wine. The alcohol is perhaps ill-advised given his current situation, but I don't protest. Instead, I loop my arms around his neck and enjoy the comfort of feeling safe against him.

"Who the fuck was that, Hades? A paid assassin?"

"A one-night stand, from many moons ago. But she's convinced she's an ex-girlfriend. And a jilted one, at that."

I must roll my mouth into a concerned pucker because he adds, "You don't have to worry about her, little nymph. She's banned for good."

"Why wasn't she already banned?" I ask.

It's a petty question, and I know it. Hades gives me a forgiving smile.

"Because I am entirely too benevolent. Fatal flaw, I suppose."

"Well, luckily now you have me to advise you on such matters."

As I swirl my fingers in the soft hair at the base of his neck, my teasing sobers.

"What did you mean when you said I was a queen?"

He kisses me in response. Once. Twice. By the third, his tongue is slipping into my mouth and scrambling my thoughts. It isn't an answer, but I realize I don't have enough fight left in me to mind. We stay like this, nursing each other's wounds, and only break apart when the doctor arrives.

"You don't have a concussion," she announces following her examination. "But you may have one hell of a headache later. Possibly some bruising. Ice would be best."

Hades nods as if he expected this. He scoops a few cubes from his drink, plops them into a beverage napkin, and presses it against his temple.

"Happy?"

The doctor smirks, giving Hades a hearty pat on the shoulder. "I'll have a server send over more. In the meantime, enjoy yourself."

When I try to get up and retrieve the fresh ice myself, Hades holds my legs in place where they're draped across his lap, stroking my thigh.

"Stay. Your closeness is critical to my wellbeing," he murmurs against my hair.

"I don't feel as though you're taking this seriously."

"I feel as though you're taking it *too* seriously." He dips his hand into his drink again, retrieving another ice cube.

"In fact, you're so hot and bothered, I think you need to cool off."

I gasp out a laugh as he touches the ice to my neck. A shock of cold drips down my chest as he drags the cube down the curve of my shoulder, along the hollows of my collarbones. I thread my fingers into his hair with a sigh, drawing his mouth close to mine.

"What are you doing?" I murmur against his lips.

"Isn't it obvious? I'm cooling you off."

"You're supposed to be resting."

"The doctor didn't say I need rest. She said I needed ice. Which is here." He breaks away long enough to extend a grateful hand to the approaching server. "Cristos, my good man. Thank you."

There is now an entire bucket of ice sitting beside us. Instead of placing it against his laceration, he snags another piece and runs it between the swell of my breasts. I gasp again at the shock of cold. A bead of water rolls down to my belly button.

The next he circles around my nipples, one after another, until they feel pinched tight. He replaces the cold with his warm mouth, flicking his tongue over the sensitive peaks. I lean into his touch with a moan.

He snags a fresh cube and dips between my thighs, stroking up and down across my clit. When it's gone, he replaces the cold with his warm palm, pressing the heel of his hand hard against me, grinding slowly up and down.

"You make me feel so dirty," I whisper against his lips. "I love it."

"I love it, too."

My chest swells. I know it isn't *love*, exactly—this thing between us. Lust seems more likely. And yet...

"Hello, lovebirds," Juno says. Her announcement is punctuated with the jostle of cushions as she plops onto the sofa beside us. "I hear I missed quite the show. If I'd known it was going to come to blows, I would've invited Ares. He does love a good fight."

"You have impeccable timing today, sister," Hades drawls in that patiently annoyed tone he seemingly always uses with Juno.

"Yes, well," she says, unbothered. "I've come to tell you I'm headed home. Zefs is remorseful. He claims he's going to repent. I figure I'm in for some grade A groveling. But I wanted to thank you for your message to him. Whatever you said, it worked."

Hades shrugs. "I only told him divorces are expensive, and did he really want to give half of everything he owns to –"

She elbows him hard, and he breaks into laughter.

"You dare to strike an injured man!" he protests.

Juno's eyes turn to slits, entirely unsympathetic. "This is probably how you got yourself injured in the first place. That devilish tongue of yours."

She hooks an arm around his neck and drags him into a hug. Given that I'm currently draped across his lap, this action involves me as well. Juno kisses the side of his face, then mine, before releasing us.

"I love you both. Behave yourselves," she says. "Oh! And before I forget."

She digs around in her handbag, producing a small tincture bottle and waggling it between us in seriousness.

"Birth control. I'm not sure what—or *who*—you have planned while you're here, but I know how things tend to go. Anyway, this is from our new naturals line. It works impeccably with the body, not against it, and it rated very highly on taste. Focus groups have gone nuts over this pomegranate flavor! Anyway, take it tonight, then once a month with the new moon should keep things on track. Or you know, just however long you need it."

My head is spinning for a moment, and I stammer, "I thought you were a marriage counselor?"

Juno rolls her eyes. "Among other things. Can anyone afford not to diversify their income in this economy?"

Hades inclines his head. "Juno is the CEO of Hera Clinic. They specialize in family planning and—"

Juno waves a hand, running through the rest like it's all boilerplate. "—and birthing centers, women's health, family counseling services, blah blah blah. She knows all this, Hades. You don't have to mansplain it to her."

I do in fact know about Hera Clinic. *Everyone* knows about Hera Clinic. In terms of power players, she's right up there with my mom; they've each got their respective markets cornered. I get all my annual check-ups there. It's where I went to get my required screenings to be eligible to cross the river. Hell, I'm pretty sure I was *born* at one of those clinics. The credentials give me some reassurance, though, and I take the bottle from her with a gracious nod.

"Thank you."

"Don't mention it," she shrugs. "And don't ever go to bed angry. I've never followed it, but I hear it's excellent relationship advice."

With another motherly look, she sweeps herself up and struts toward the main exit. Hades returns his smile to me, tucking his nose against my neck and sliding his fingers between my legs.

"Now. Where were we?"

When I first arrived here, I believed the primary focus of the parties on this side of the Styx was sex. Admittedly, since then, I've enjoyed plenty of it, and—given that Hades is still playing this game of bringing me to the edge and leaving me wet and wanting—I plan to have much more.

But I was wrong to believe it was *only* sex.

The more comfortable I become, the more that I'm able to see the variety of ways people come to enjoy themselves here. Some sit at card tables, smoking cigars and betting on games of chance. Some seem to be living in a fairytale world of sensation: finger-painting each other's bodies, sucking down what looks to be Kool-Aid from ridiculously tall plastic cups, dancing like they can feel the very air caress their skin. Others enjoy dinner and drinks, as if this is any swanky and exclusive hotel lobby back in Olympus.

And music, there's plenty of music. The bass-heavy DJ beats from earlier have given way to more intimate acoustic sets befitting of laughter and conversation. It has collected around us in an easy, organic way, until our small lounge area is brimming with animated stories, off-color jokes, and a man playing the most beautiful songs I've ever heard on a small stringed instrument.

If not for the fact that I'm wearing a body harness and my tits are still on display, this Saturday evening almost feels normal. Comfortable, even. Hades has one arm draped around me, while he argues animatedly about the details of a recollection from Dionysus. On my other side is a new acquaintance, who is equally as enraptured with the music as I am. I find myself leaning my shoulder against hers, following her dreamy gaze to the musician.

"Is it some sort of harp?" I wonder aloud.

"A lyre," she replies. "And it's said the gods themselves cannot play it as well as him. Orpheus, I think his name is."

"It's truly enchanting," I say. "Does he play here often?"

The way the man is perched at the edge of our group, strumming intently, gives him the vibe of a hired lounge singer. I'm surprised he doesn't have a tip jar nearby. I don't have any money, but I'm captivated in a way that makes me want to find an ATM and retrieve something to give him.

The woman leans in confidentially. "I heard he's been here for weeks. He came to win back his wife."

I furrow my brow. "Oh. Did she run away?"

"No. She died," she whispers. "I heard they went on one of those new age backpacking honeymoons, and somewhere in the backcountry she got bitten by a snake. They said he tried to carry her to safety, but the poison made it to her heart before he was able to get help."

"Oh my god. That's terrible."

"A tragedy," she agrees.

Sympathy swells within me. This guy is young—maybe close to my age—but I realize now there's a sadness in his eyes that makes him look much older. I wonder if being on this side of the river all this time has taken a toll on his health.

"Can people do that?" I ask. "Bring someone back?"

She shrugs. "I wouldn't know."

As the conversation shifts, I nestle my way back into the crook of Hades's arm, suddenly grateful to have him next to me in this world so full of loss. I feel the vibration of laughter in his chest as he listens to yet another of Dionysus's wild stories, and I'm quickly sucked in as well. He might be a shameless lush, but few people can keep the wine flowing and the stories going quite like Dionysus.

It's not until some time later, when the conversation lulls and the sounds of the strings dance back into my consciousness, that I put a hand to Hades's chest, gingerly tracing the buttons of his shirt.

"Do you know him?" I ask softly. "The musician, I mean."

"I know he's very talented," he says.

"Do you also know he's looking for his wife?"

There's a slight tick in his jaw. "I know he thinks the rules of life and death do not apply to her, yes."

"You don't want to see them reunited?"

Hades releases a long sigh through his nose. "It's not as simple as that."

I consider the chaos that would be unleashed if suddenly people heard they could bargain with death. The mothers and fathers, friends and lovers that would line up to barter and beg. Still, my heart breaks a little, especially as the music the man is coaxing from his strings takes on the purest sound of longing.

"She's here, though?"

"Not here. The dead aren't allowed in the palace. If I had to guess, she's somewhere along the banks of the river Cocytus, lamenting her lost love." There's genuine sympathy behind his eyes now. "The young almost never go easy. So much life left unlived. But some would argue there's never enough time. Not for any of us."

The aching reality that I'll be leaving here tomorrow creeps between my ribs. I shake my head, willing the feeling away.

"I wish there was something we could do," I say, almost to myself.

Hades threads his fingers between mine, giving me an assessing look. "If you were queen here, ruling over the entire Underworld, what would you do?"

I chew the inside of my lip, considering. "I would let him go. Let him journey to the river of lamenting, or whatever you called it. Let him see if he can really do it."

"You'd have me send a mortal man into the Underworld armed with nothing but love and his lyre?" he smirks. "You think that'd be enough?"

I cast my gaze back to the young man with the hollow eyes and the deft fingers, playing music like his very life—or perhaps, his *wife*—depends on it. I imagine it's the same determination that he summoned when he carried her hours through the backcountry, snakebitten and doomed from the start.

The emotion that swells within me sends chills down my arms, stings at my eyes. I give him a wistful smile. "Yes."

8

The longer I am here in this kingdom of the dead, the more acutely I learn that there are many ways to worship.

Some worship with words: whispered pleas, joyful praise, murmured prayers.

Some worship through faith: acts of service and selflessness, unquestioned devotion.

Others worship with their bodies, their flesh, giving themselves up to the kind of ecstasy that feels like communion with a higher power.

When I am led to the altar of Hades, I am unsure which kind is expected of me, or which kind I can expect to receive.

The marble statue looms large on the stage. A patio space sprawls in front of it, complete with winding water features and an ornate fountain. Small, candlelit tables are scattered around it, as if this is the kind of place people gather for dinner theater. I swallow past the tightness in my throat that only increases when it occurs to me that tonight I'm the entertainment.

"I thought you had to be a virgin to be sacrificed."

I try to keep my tone light, but my nerves betray me, and I have to place my hands on my hips to keep them from trembling.

"We're not sacrificing your virginity," Hades says. "We're sacrificing that good girl persona you said you were so tired of tending. The one who wants people to think she doesn't get herself off thinking about getting tied up and punished and pleasured. Unless you've changed your mind?"

I glance at the people milling about, wondering if I'm prepared to be completely on display in front of them. I could leave now and go back to my privileged, easy life, and no one would be any the wiser. In general, what happens across the Styx stays across the Styx. The likelihood that any activities in which I've partaken so far would get back to the company I tend to keep seems slim.

But if I get up on that altar? Sacrifice myself to Hades? Well, that's another story entirely—the kind people get excited to tell.

On either side of the statue are two arched arbors, lined with creeping vines and exotic flowers. Now that we're closer, I spy cuffs hanging from the top beams. My pulse ticks up a notch.

I realize there has proven to be a method to Hades's madness. Because I'm horny. *Really* fucking horny. The girl I normally pretend to be would never dream of fulfilling this fantasy, least of all in front of an audience, but I've been teased and toyed with on and off for hours.

Getting dressed up in this sexy outfit.

Getting licked and sucked and fingered by Cerberus.

Getting led around this party like Hades's little pet, that he periodically strokes until she's begging.

I bite my bottom lip, gently clutching the buttery fabric of his shirt into my fists.

"You said if I go up there, I can have your cock," I remind him.

He tips his head side to side, noncommittal. "Eventually."

When he gives me a mischievous smile, I match it with one of my own.

The lights dramatically dim, and an emcee takes the lighted stage, which only serves to hype the crowd. My anxiety grows with the swelling sound of chatter and noise and anticipation, and I pour myself another glass of wine from the bottle we haven't yet finished. It's gone in a series of gulps.

"That's our cue," Hades says, taking up my leash.

He guides us up the stairs, prancing me across the front of the altar like a prized pony. Under the shining spotlights, I feel my tits give a subtle bounce with every step. The second they see us, the crowd noise climbs.

Anyone in this place who hasn't already gathered at the base of the altar or crowded into the balconies surrounding the atrium is most certainly heading this way now. Hades brings us to a stop in front of a standing microphone, giving genial waves and nods to his throngs of fans.

"Thank you."

His voice surrounds us, dark and decadent through the speakers.

"Every evening here is indeed itself a treat, but tonight I have a very *special* treat."

He pauses to gaze at me, running his thumb along my jaw for emphasis. A hint of a smile plays across my lips at the delicate gesture.

"And this," he continues, "is a treat we're planning to share with you. Because this horny little princess has agreed to sacrifice herself to me—publicly, on this altar, for our collective enjoyment."

Applause roars, louder now than before.

Hidden from the audience, Hades slides his hand over the curve of my backside, giving it a gentle, reassuring squeeze. Outwardly, he gives a benign smile. He quiets the chaos with a single lift of his hand.

"We only need to get a few important items squared away first." He turns to me. "Persephone."

For the first time, I hear my delicate voice sweep through the room.

"Hades."

A few quiet chuckles ripple through the crowd.

"You know we don't take hostages here. Can you reassure these good people that you're doing this of your own free will?"

I bite into my smile, licking my lips before I draw them closer to the microphone. "I submit myself to you willingly, yes."

A few wolf whistles rise up.

"And you consent to be fucked, however I say you'll be fucked?"

A blush burns across my cheeks, more intense than the heat of the spotlights bearing down on us.

"Yes."

"And you'll enjoy this?"

I give a breathy, nervous laugh. I'm relieved when a few in the audience match my energy. "Very much, I hope."

"And you know that you have the power to stop this at any time by saying your safe word?"

"I do."

"And you understand that if you can't use your mouth to speak for any reason that any noise or action made in a rapid series of three will grant your immediate freedom?"

Images of exactly how I might be unable to use my mouth flit through my mind.

"Yes, I understand."

His eyes flash with excitement. "Good. Take off your skirt."

The shift in his tone is abrupt, and it sends a chill of anticipation through me. I meet his gaze with my heart in my throat.

"If I have to do it for you, princess, there will be consequences."

A tittering sound of amusement shifts through the crowd, heightening my awareness that we're being watched.

With a shimmy of my hips, my skirt falls to the floor, and there's nothing left to hide behind. The strappy garters of the body harness stretch seductively down to the thigh cuffs. My pussy is on full display, and it's already growing hot with arousal. I instinctively tuck my arms across my torso in an attempt to cover myself.

This warrants a sharp slap on my ass. "No hiding."

I force my hands down to my sides.

I am naked, on a stage, being ordered around like a sex slave. And I am undeniably terrified and excited about this.

"Sorry, sir," I murmur. "Habit."

Hades uses the leash to bring my face close to his. My lips part instinctively, desperate for a kiss, as if it could act as a balm to the reprimand.

"I think I'm going to have to break you of those bad habits."

His lips brush mine for the barest moment, and then he turns away, breaking into an easy stride. I stumble in my quick attempt to follow. Hades uses the leash to guide me to the nearest arbor.

"Arms up," he says.

When I comply, the firm orbs of my breasts lift seductively, crowded together from the position. With a single gesture of his hand, a duo in flowy, cream-colored robes appear—literally appear—as if summoned from the shadows. They look almost ethereal, like otherworldly priests or priestesses, here to do Hades's bidding. He watches as they move to either side of me, simultaneously hooking a soft, velvet-lined cuff snugly around each of my wrists, pinning them overhead.

"How do they feel?" he questions.

I give them a testing tug. "Good."

"Good. Now spread your legs."

I do as he says, but he shakes his head.

"Wider."

My pulse jumps as I obey. When he's satisfied with my stance, the robed devotees crouch to latch a cuff around each ankle. Only when I'm fully restrained does Hades come closer, unclipping the leash from my collar.

"Do you like being tied up, princess? Spread open wide in front of all these people?"

My voice betrays how I'm trembling. "Yes, sir."

"Mm. Maybe we can show them how much you like it."

The first two altar attendants have disappeared, but another materializes, dressed in those same flowing robes. Her golden hair falls over her face as she bows at Hades's side, offering him an open leather case. I strain to see what all is inside but only catch glimpses: a cat o'nine tails, a ball gag, nipple clamps, a double-edged dildo. I'm relieved when he selects a simple vibrator.

He drags the lifeless toy over my lips, down my throat, between my breasts, teasing each nipple in a way that makes me aware that I am defenseless to stop him. A desperate vulnerability aches through me as he drags it further down, wiggling it against my clit. I sigh a little at the contact, and he smiles.

"Your slutty pussy is already so wet," he notes, stroking slowly. "Do you want me to turn it on?"

A shiver runs through me.

"Yes." I swallow. "Please."

The vibration hits me like a jolt, and I cry out a moan. The cuffs around my wrists are tight as I attempt to keep myself upright.

"Is this what you want, princess? You want me to rub your greedy little cunt and show them how well you come?"

My face burns, but I continue to sigh out affirmations. Every nerve in my body is already alive and reaching for any pleasure he'll give me. He works the toy against my slick, swollen clit. My eyes slide closed at the sheer pleasure of it.

The sting against my breasts comes quick.

"Oh!" I yelp.

My eyes fly open, and I see the culprit: another altar attendant has brought Hades the cat o'nine tails. He grips it in one hand as he pleasures me with the other, dragging the soft ends of the whip along the contours of my breasts before notching the handle under my chin.

"Eyes on me, princess. I want you to watch me ruin you."

My nipples pinch tight as I press my tits against the teasing touch of leather. He grinds the vibrator against me again. My moan is long and low.

Another stinging slap lands on my tits. I swear as my eyes pop open, wondering how I lost my focus enough to make the same mistake twice.

"I'm sorry, sir," I say, as he gently caresses the red marks on my breasts. "It just feels so... good..."

"Don't apologize." His voice is as sharp as the lashes he's given me. "I want you to show all these people what a horny girl you are. How much you love to get pleasured and punished. Can you do that for me, princess?"

"Yes," I mewl.

Another swipe across my tits. "Yes what?"

"Yes, sir," I grit out.

I rock my hips against his touch, too drunk on lust to care how this looks. My hands cling to the tethers of the cuffs, relying on the strength of my arms as my legs turn to Jello. The sound of my moans surrounds us, amplified by the hanging microphones that have caught every word of this exchange.

"Please," I beg. "Please, can I come?"

He swipes another sting across me, and my eyes snap open again. My vision blurs, and I realize they're tearing from the overwhelming sensations. Heat has pooled between my trembling legs, and I grind my hips faster. He notches up the vibration.

"Holy *fuck*," I breathe. "Hades... I'm going to come. Please."

"How bad do you want it?"

Suddenly, the sensation of the vibrator is gone. He is holding it a couple of inches away so that I have to jut out my hips in an attempt to bridge the gap. The restraints make this almost impossible.

I whimper. "I can't reach."

"You're sure?"

He waggles it, and I thrust forward without success. Again, and again, until I'm tugging so tight against the cuffs that my wrists ache.

"I can't... Hades... Please... I..."

When I manage to make contact, my brain goes black with lust.

"Oh my god," I moan.

I'm bucking my hips in an open and obscene way, desperate to get myself off.

"Oh, what a perfect slut you are."

Fuck. Yes. Fuck. Yes...

I struggle against my restraints, thrusting my hips faster, chasing the sensation to the very edge.

He snugs the handle of the whip under my chin.

"Look at me when I let you come, princess."

I scream out another cry, locking in on the absolute animal intensity in his gaze.

"There it is," he purrs.

The release I've been chasing all day surges through me in waves that rack my body. I sob at the pleasure. When my eyes slide closed, Hades swipes another warning across my stinging breasts.

"Oh!" I wail. But despite my protests, it only seems to intensify the orgasm. My entire body is thrumming. My legs completely collapse, and I'm left clinging to the cuffs, twisting against them.

Four of the flowy figures emerge from the shadows of the stage. They release my ankles and wrists from the arbor with practiced precision. Hades catches me before I can crumple to the floor, hauling me over his shoulder and carrying me to the marble altar. The stone is cool against my hot, welted skin as he bends me over it.

"Have you had enough yet?"

He runs his fingers up and down the dripping wetness of my slit, and I moan. I haven't had anywhere close to enough. The climax only intensified how much I want him.

"Please," I beg.

The table is tall and wide enough that when he steps on the other side, his hips are level with my face.

He removes his shirt with a smooth roll of muscle. When he unzips his pants, his magnificent cock springs free. He gives it a tentative stroke before threading his fingers into my hair and tipping my tear-streaked gaze up to meet his. He rubs the thick head across my lips, which part for him instinctively.

"You want me to fuck you?" he teases.

"Yes," I breathe.

I reach for him open mouthed like a hungry little bird. I lick the salty bead of arousal with an eager hum, swirling my tongue around the tip. He knots his grip in my hair as I take him in.

"Yes, *sir*," he corrects. "Maybe if I fuck your smart mouth you'll learn some manners."

The truth is I love the feel of him in my mouth. I love the way his breath goes desperate when I flick my tongue along the sensitive underside. The way he groans when I take him so deep I choke.

When he withdraws, my chin and throat are glistening with my own saliva. He fists his cock and strokes my hair.

"Mm. You suck my cock like such a dirty fucking girl. I want you to show them how good you are. Can you do that for me?"

I wonder if he knows in this current state that I'll agree to anything he wants. I wonder if everyone watching us knows.

Because I will.

Because I *am*. Desperate and horny and agreeing that I'll suck as many cocks as he wants if it means he'll fuck me.

"Yes, sir."

In the front row, there's an attractive guy who has been stroking himself, watching us. Hades motions him up the stairs. He drags his thumb across my bottom lip as the guy approaches us, peeling off his shirt to reveal lean muscles.

"I couldn't help but notice you're enjoying the show," Hades says to him. He reaches out and wraps his other hand around the guy's hard length, pumping slowly. The man's knees momentarily buckle.

"Very much, sir," the guy breathes.

"Such a nice, hard cock. Doesn't he have a nice cock, princess?" Hades says, stroking the thick shaft. "Don't you want to put it in your mouth?"

I lick my lips. "Mhmm."

It's shockingly sexy, watching this scenario play out right in front of me. Hades's guiding the man's swollen tip against my tongue. My wrapping my lips around the satisfying thickness. I find myself drinking in the desperation of it. The three of us, all so obviously horny and ready for release.

"That's it, princess. Suck his cock nice and slow for me."

The man tips his head back with a groan, and Hades kisses the beautiful plane of his throat. He palms his hips, guiding him into an easy rhythm.

It's a new kink completely unlocked: my man with another man. I could drown in the stunning masculinity of it.

I find myself reaching forward, gripping each of them in one hand, wondering if I've ever imagined a world where I would be sucking two men off at once before.

I don't get the chance to find out.

"I didn't tell you to *touch* his cock," Hades warns. "I told you to suck it."

In a quick motion, he gathers my hands behind me and clips the cuffs together at the small of my back. When I'm restrained, he drags his fingers down my spine and over my ass, sending chills through me.

"Do you want more, Persephone?" Hades asks, positioning himself behind me. I moan around the cock in my mouth.

Then I feel the leather handle of the cat o'nine tails slap against my inner thighs, spreading them wider. He rubs it against my opening, pressing into me with satisfying fullness, while the man in front of me fists my hair, driving deeper.

It feels good—too good—but I want Hades. The warm girth of him, filling me up. As if reading my mind, he says, "Make that cock come, and I'll fuck you myself."

I moan, sucking harder while he works the leather handle in and out of my pussy. Wetness drips down my thighs, and saliva dribbles down my chin, and I feel the man in my mouth getting harder, hear his breathing growing ragged.

He's close, and I realize I will gladly choke on his cock if it means I can have Hades inside of me. The thought makes me delirious with need.

"Holy fuck," the guy breathes, gripping my hair.

"Isn't her mouth magnificent?" Hades says, massaging my clit. "Don't you want to come all over her pretty face?"

"Fuck, yes," he groans in agreement.

My own orgasm is building, and I can't ask permission. I twist against the bind around my wrists, hoping to signal him somehow.

"You're going to come again, princess?"

I groan loud enough to be heard over the slick, sucking sounds. He has me right at the edge, and suddenly the cock in my mouth twitches hard.

"Open your mouth, Persephone," Hades commands. "Nice and wide. Let us see that cock come all over your face."

Hot cum is spilling across my open mouth, my cheeks, my chin. My lips feel swollen and stretched, but I still manage to moan as Hades brings me to the edge. He withdraws his touch at the last possible moment.

"Please," I pant, licking the sticky salt off my lips. "Fuck me, please."

"You haven't had enough yet?"

A firm slap lands across my ass. My face burns.

"No."

He laughs.

"You're such a perfect—"

Slap.

"—horny—"

Slap, slap, slap.

"—slut."

I cry out as he caresses the stinging skin. I am pleasure, and I am agony, and I need him inside me more than I've ever needed anything.

"I'm so fucking horny. I want your cock so bad, please."

"I love it when you beg."

He slides himself up and down my pussy until I whimper.

"You know I should make you suck every cock in this room for being such a greedy girl. Maybe I will."

He snaps his fingers, and two more attendants appear. They shed their robes as they cross the stage, pure devotion already glimmering in their eyes. One is a bronzed woman wearing a large black strap on. The other is a man wearing a cock ring, which has his dick hard and swollen. The woman runs a dainty hand down my back, over the curve of my ass, positioning herself behind me as the man fists my hair and turns my cum-streaked face up. I moan as I take them both, delirious with need.

"Mmm, yes," Hades hums.

He circles us, taking in this scene from every angle. It's only a few moments later that the unmistakable tickle of leather slides across my backside. Chills run through my body, hardening my nipples as they rub against the cool marble with every thrust of the woman behind me.

"Have you had enough yet?" Hades asks.

My mouth is full, but I groan out a sound that I hope resembles, *No.*

A sharp sting lands across my ass, and I choke out a cry. Pleasure mingles with pain, and the effect is intoxicating.

"Are you sure?" he asks, tickling the tails against my skin again.

I groan as the man fucks my mouth harder, chasing his own release. The woman teases my clit with her delicate fingers, and my whole body trembles, on the verge of coming apart.

"You want him to come on your face, princess? Number two of two hundred?"

Something in me threatens to break, but I attempt to nod around the furious thrusts. The man pulls out at the last possible moment, letting his release coat my mouth, my cheeks, my hair. Hades swipes another sting across my ass, leaving me sobbing or moaning or begging, or some delirious combination of all three.

The dildo slides out of me with a slick sound, and the attendants disappear. I am throbbing and empty. I lay my sticky cheek against the cool table, blinking back tears. Hades crouches beside me, smoothing my sweaty hair away from my face so he can search my gaze.

"Do you still want my cock?"

My voice is a trembling whimper. "Yes."

"You think you deserve it?"

My bottom lip quivers, and he drags his thumb across it as I use all of my strength to nod.

"Why's that, princess?"

I lick my swollen lips, tasting the salt. "Because I'm yours."

His mouth twitches into a villainous smirk. "Because you're mine."

He draws himself to his full height and walks around the table again.

"This ass is mine?" he teases, dragging the leather across it.

My voice is a hoarse plea. "Yes."

He swipes another sting across it. I hear his zipper, and I instinctively spread my legs wider.

"This slutty pussy is mine?" he growls. He rubs himself up and down my slit, and a sob escapes me.

"Yes. Fuck. *Yes.*"

When he presses inside me, I shudder out a gasp of relief. Tears well in my eyes, and a tingly wave of warmth surges through me.

"Oh god, yes. Fuck me. Please."

And finally, he does. He fucks me with smooth, possessive strokes, with his palms spread wide around my hips so that he can tug me back to meet his thrusts. The stone table is slick with my sweat, and I slide back and forth against it.

"You're so fucking wet," he laughs. "You love getting used like this, don't you?"

Yes. Yes. Yes.

Maybe I say it out loud, or maybe I'm just moaning incoherent sounds, the chorus over the steady slap of skin on skin as he drives me toward the edge. With one cheek pressed against the cool marble, hot tears of pleasure slide over the bridge of my nose, down my face.

How many times can I come before I lose my mind? How many times can he bring me to the edge before I break?

"You are a fucking goddess, Persephone. You are my queen. You want to come all over my cock, don't you, Your Highness?"

This new endearment twists through me, drawing the threads of tension tighter. I'm hoarse as I beg, chanting in a language I barely understand, the kind of words one can only *feel*. And the feel of his orgasm pulsing inside me is hot and molten, tipping me over the edge with him. It is the pure ecstasy I've been chasing all day. It is a pleasure so deep I wonder if it's going to swallow me whole.

I am undone.

I am only acutely aware as he kisses between my shoulder blades that he is unclasping my wrists and sitting me to face the rapt audience and blinding spotlights. I blink into their brightness, into the hungry faces. Until now, I've almost forgotten they're here. Where the other people went after they played their part in this, I have no clue.

Hades sweeps my hair over my shoulders, spreads my knees wide, traces the outline of my body with reverent sweeps of his fingers. The featherlight touches make my pussy twitch with aftershocks of pleasure, and he drinks in the sight of me like a man dying of thirst. When he kisses me deeply, I melt against him with a groan.

He caresses my swollen lips. Licks at the lines of cum on my throat. Kisses across the welts on my breasts until I feel like butter: warm and melty.

Then he sinks to his knees in front of me. When he buries his face between my thighs, I cry out again, threading my fingers into his hair.

They all watch him worship me. Every wide pair of eyes, greedy for the details. The way he lovingly sucks at my clit, dips his tongue into my opening, licking up all of our juices with humming satisfaction. The way my head tips back with an open-mouthed sigh, breathing out his name.

Over.

And over.

My entire body buzzes with a new sensation, and I recognize it as an intoxicating rush.

Power.

It's seductive, and this time I don't close my eyes. I want to watch every second of this man—this king, this *god*—kneeling in front of me, looking up at me, feasting on me like I'm his last meal.

Maybe I come again. Maybe I never stopped. Or maybe this is something else altogether. A pleasure that vibrates in every cell of my being, as if my body has been coaxed over the edge so many times that every stroke of his tongue feels like ecstasy.

When he stands, I can still feel our slippery spend on my thighs and the sticky lines of cum on my face. He doesn't clean me off. Instead, he scoops me into his arms and carries me through the hushed crowd, cum-soaked and tear-streaked and completely wrecked.

Entirely reborn.

They bow at our feet as we pass.

9

As a girl, I always wondered how naive those cartoon princesses had to be to fall madly in love with the hero in the span of three days. As a woman, though, with Hades gently washing me in our private Roman spa and carrying me to bed feeling clean and new, I wonder if those princesses were onto something.

"You are more perfect than I ever dreamed you would be," he says against my temple.

"Is that why you invited me here?" I ask, my tone teasing and soft. "Was I your daydream?"

"Of sorts," he admits. "I saw you once. When I was across the river on business."

Surprise coaxes a smile from me. "Really? I didn't know you ever went across the river."

"I don't make it a habit, admittedly. It was probably one of those meetings where I sat there and looked 'disappointed.'"

I chortle, waiting for more of this story, but he pauses, as if that might be all he has to say. I've noticed this about him, his tendency to withhold. I expect this to be one of those times as well. Then, I hear his wistful smile.

"It was a miserable day," he says. "The rain was coming down in sheets. Most people were skittering in and out of buildings like rats. But then I passed you on the street. And I'd never seen anyone so… alive. Your bright eyes. Your playful smile. Your hair, damp even though you carried an umbrella. You barely seemed to care that it was raining. And you stopped to literally smell the roses.

"I'm serious. They were a bright burst of pink, growing along the chain-link fence surrounding one of your back-alley gardens. You lingered long enough to pull a pair of garden snips from your purse and keep one of the blooms. You stuck it behind your ear, and I couldn't help but wonder if you even bothered to trim the thorns. And you saw me. And you smiled."

I can almost picture it. The dull day and bright blooms. The smell of rain and damp earth. And yet the memory exists just out of my reach.

"When was this?" I ask, mystified.

"A few years ago."

I choke out a laugh. "*Years?*"

"I'm rather skilled at waiting for what I want. Some say it heightens the pleasure of the experience."

I sink into a satisfied smirk, thinking about how he waited all day to fuck me, though his cock had been a hard ridge straining against his pants.

"So that's it, then? I smiled at you, and you wanted to take your pleasure from me?" I tease.

I hope my attempt at humor will calm the way my heart is thudding wild in my chest.

"No, little nymph. When you smiled at me, I had this sudden urge to give you everything. The moon. The stars. A hundred lifetimes of happiness. Things that aren't even mine to give."

My voice is small in the dark. "Why? Why me?"

He swells with a breath, snugging me ever-so-slightly closer with one arm as he tucks the other behind his head.

"My whole existence, I've always felt like people don't really *see* me. They see what they want to see. Power. Death. Sin. Lust. They either want to bargain with me, cheat me, or fuck me. Or they ignore me altogether, because they can't face the fact that one day everyone on this planet will take their last breath. They offer each other empty platitudes in the face of grief, as if they could distance themselves from the idea of me. But when you looked at me that day, it's the same way you look at me now. I feel like you really see me—see all the parts of me—and you aren't afraid."

My chest swells with a feeling I can't place. Its warm, hazy sweetness laces my words.

"I'm not."

"And," he continues conspiratorially, "I had a feeling about you. That your milk-and-honey skin was soft but also... hungry. Aching to be touched."

"Well," I say, kissing his full bottom lip. "I do love the way you touch me."

I thread my fingers through his, sobering.

"Why didn't you talk to me that day? You could have invited me here then."

He wets his lips. "It all happened too fast. You saw me, and smiled, and a big gust took your umbrella straight into the street. Without thinking you turned, and—"

I shift upright, suddenly remembering the bone deep panic of that moment. All of the details come into clear focus then: my misstep, my reaching without thinking, the sound of tires, the spray of water, my twisted umbrella lying in the street. And the inexplicable pull that kept me inches from death. I never understood how my momentum landed me on my ass on the sidewalk instead of in front of that car.

I blink at him in the dark. "It was you."

He's quiet, and it's all the answer I need. Suddenly, questions are pouring out of me.

"Why didn't you stay? Why didn't you say something? You could've said something. We could've –"

"Persephone." When he says my name, it has a gentle, calming effect. He smooths a thumb across the furrow in my brow. "I told you when you first arrived here: I ruin things. I will ruin you. Even that day, I convinced myself I distracted you somehow, that it was my fault you almost –"

"No. It was the wind. You *saved* me," I argue. "And you eventually invited me here anyway!"

He gives me a patient smile. "That I did."

"What changed?"

"You."

The word is a deep, smooth rumble in his chest like faraway thunder. I search his eyes for an explanation.

"I don't understand."

"That day on the street, I met a very good girl. One who felt like she had the world in her pocket, who only wanted everything she already had. She would never have gotten on that ferry. And if she had, I would have broken her. And I never would have forgiven myself for it.

"But the person I left that coin for? She was a *woman*. One who was suddenly so very tired of trying to be perfect, who felt trapped by the life she'd been given but had never been allowed to really, fully live. Not on her terms, at least. Not how she wanted. She was always trying to be something for someone, everything for everyone, and I knew that this woman—if she got on that boat—was not someone who could be broken easily. Or she already would've been."

I realize I'm trembling, as if the echoes of the truth are vibrating through my veins. "How could you possibly have known all that?"

"Maybe that's what I do," he teases. "Sit here in my big palace across the river and know things."

I sink further into the luxury of his arms and pillows and linens, drawing lazy circles on his chest. The idea of getting on the ferry and heading home tomorrow feels incomprehensible. The knowledge that I won't be able to hear his heartbeat when I lay my head on his chest, breathing in the smoke-and-spice scent of his skin as I near sleep. The terror that I will never feel this good again.

"I want to stay," I whisper.

Shadows dance through the room as the jasmine breeze sways through the curtains leading to the balcony. His chest rises and falls a few times as I await his response.

"Eventually people are going to realize you're gone," he says, tracing the line of my hip, the valley of my waist. "And when your mother finds out you're here, I can't imagine she'll be happy about it."

It feels so selfish, but I can't help it. I hear myself say, "I don't care if she's happy. *I'm* happy."

It's not that shiny, surface happiness that feels like the posed photos on my socials. This one is deeper: a contentment that has settled into my very soul.

"What about your gardens?"

I think of the small urban spaces, already nearing the end of their seasons. Most of the tomatoes and peppers and beans have already been plucked from their vines. The sunflowers will soon shed their seeds. The carrots and beets will all be uprooted with the first cool breaths of fall.

"They can get along fine without me. Especially now. It's about to be off season. Planning season. And if you allow me a laptop, I can do all of that remotely."

I hear the hint of amusement in his voice. "And where will you tell them you've gone?"

"Abroad," I shrug. He exhales a quiet laugh at the way my voice goes up at the end, like maybe it's a question. "What? It could work."

"They'll think I've kidnapped you. This is how rumors get started. People talk."

"I don't care. Let them talk."

"Stay for now," he says. "Stay for the winter, even, if you're so adamant. But in the Spring, when it's time to sow new seeds and tend to your gardens, I have a feeling you'll want to go home."

My limbs are heavy with the need for sleep, but I climb on top of him. His cock stirs as I caress his mouth with mine, drawing him into a sensual kiss and rolling my hips against him until he's hard enough to slip inside me. I sigh with relief as I sink all the way against him, reveling in the feeling of being filled up so completely.

"Maybe I am home."

The days and nights across the river bleed into each other. When Hades isn't busy attending to matters of the Under-world, he lavishes me with his attention. We take long sunrise walks around the grounds and soothing sunset swims in the spas. We picnic along the edge of the Elysian fields, where Hades undresses me under the shade of one of the sprawling trees, feasting on me in the open air, under the low-sweeping, fairytale branches that form a cozy canopy. In the afternoons, I curl across his lap as we read books on the balcony. And in the evenings, I put on long, flowing dresses tailored for me by the skilled Arachne, who knows exactly how to accentuate my attributes and make me feel like a princess.

"Not a princess," Hades murmurs against the back of my neck, when he hears me say this to my reflection in the full-length mirror. "A queen."

He smooths his hands up my ass, to the small of my waist, tracing his fingers down the low neckline to tease my breasts. He removes the collar and replaces it with a necklace, inlaid with jewels and boasting a beautiful pendant that sits just beneath the hollow at the center of my collarbones. I rub my fingers across it, feeling the clear emblem of Hades.

"It's beautiful," I breathe.

"Seemed more fitting than a crown," he shrugs. "Though there's one of those too, if you prefer."

We walk the winding paths of the palace until we reach the terraced, white-washed shops and restaurants and staff dwellings carved into the mountainside that remind me of glossy, magazine-worthy prints of Santorini. We have dinner at an intimate little bistro overlooking the Styx. We buy warm, flaky baklava from the bakery and eat it straight from the box as we make our way back, talking and laughing.

We make love. We stay up late. We fall asleep in a satisfied haze.

Each day after breakfast, I settle into the routine of working on the laptop Hades procured for me, and thus far I haven't had to tell my team anything beyond that I'll be "working remotely for the foreseeable future" and that I have "full faith in [their] ability to keep Bounty thriving", and that I am "available if [they] need any guidance". My mother, however, is a different story.

"Are you trying to ruin me?"

It's one of the many scathing voicemail recordings that I hear when I finally retrieve my phone from the lockbox, and I wait two full days before I bother to call her back.

"Persephone! There you are. I've been hearing terrible rumors that you were—" She lowers her voice to a scandalized whisper. "—across the river."

"They're not 'terrible rumors', Mother. It's the truth. I am across the river." I hear her sharp hiss of breath and attempt to head off whatever comes next. "But I'm also okay. Better than okay, actually. I'm perfectly safe. And I'm planning to... stay a while."

"You stupid girl. Across the river?! Do you have any idea what the media will do when they get a hold of this?"

Annoyance prickles the back of my neck. This is always the case with my mother. What will people think? How will this look? It's never, 'What do you want? How do you feel?'

The suffocating feeling I've carried around since childhood expands in my chest. I recognize it as guilt, or obligation, but now it's mingled with something sharper and less obedient.

"You've buried stories before. If it bothers you so much, I'm sure you could use your connections to bury this one as well."

She makes a low wailing sound. "Why would you do this to me, Persephone? Why?"

I sigh, struggling to find the words to explain this in terms she'll understand. "It's really not about you, Mother."

She scoffs. "Who are you to speak to me this way? I have given you *everything*. I didn't raise you to be like this!"

No, I think. *You raised me to be a content little greenhouse flower, always keeping up appearances, terrified to step out of the confines you've created for me, and you're upset I've turned out to be a wild thing that has outgrown your ability to contain me.*

"What about your garden projects?" she continues. "Are you going to abandon those, too?"

"I'm not abandoning anything. I'm still working. Business will continue like normal."

"Not if I have anything to say about it. I can cut your funding with a single word, remember that."

"And I can tell everyone you're shutting down the project because you don't care about the urban food deserts you've created with your chokehold supply chain."

"You wouldn't dare," she hisses.

"Watch me."

"Two can play this game, young lady. And keep in mind, I've been playing it much longer than you."

When the call disconnects, I'm left with an unsteadiness sinking into my stomach like a stone.

"She didn't take it well," Hades says across the table.

I place the phone face down on the surface. "No."

"She's only concerned about you."

"That's an optimistic way to look at it," I murmur.

"There's no need to start a war," he says. "Give it time."

10

War isn't in my nature. I was raised to be agreeable. My assigned task was to always be achieving, reaching, climbing some imaginary ladder, but to make it look effortless, and to always do it with a smile. As such, my goals have always come with quietly ambitious deadlines. It's as if I've always been rushing toward some finish line that's perpetually out of reach, in an effort to keep me too exhausted to consider deviating from the path.

So, I'm not saying I'm in the mood to start a war, but I'm also not saying a streak of defiance isn't coursing through me that evening when I put on the floral jacquard bustier that dazzles with vibrant hues of pomegranate red, midnight black, and Aegean blue and crowds my tits together like ripe, luscious fruit. I pair it with a short skirt, the leather collar, and lipstick so dark and red that it could never be considered modest. The thought that it would horrify my mother to know the woman she raised wants to be paraded around like a willing whore sends an added thrill through me.

I find Hades in his dressing room, adjusting his cuf-flinks. His eyes flash with intrigue when he catches my reflection in the mirror. He turns slowly, letting his gaze rake up my body. I hear the hint of a smile in his voice.

"I thought you were getting dressed for dinner."

I give a seductive shrug. "I figured we might change up the menu tonight."

"Mmm. What did you have in mind?"

"You," I say, kissing his neck, "bending me over a table and fucking me in front of all your friends."

He snags my chin, bringing my gaze to meet his. "Is that so? You know it won't be quite like last time."

"No?"

"No. Last time I was going easy on you."

A shiver of anticipation runs through me.

"What about this time? Will you go..." I grip the length of him, already stirring to attention in his pants. "...hard?"

"Don't tease me, little nymph."

"Or what?"

In a single, effortless instant, he has his hand around my throat and my back against his front. I'm met with my reflection in the mirror, wide-eyed and gasping. His free hand roams over my breasts.

"Or I'll have you on your hands and knees."

His touch trails down.

"With a cock in your mouth. And one in your ass. And one in your pussy."

He grips the heat between my legs as if he could lift me off my feet. His dark, midnight eyes bore into mine.

"You'll be so stretched full that you'll be begging they come before they rip your tight little cunt apart."

My breaths come as quick, shallow pants. Hades grazes his mouth along the shell of my ear.

"Does that excite you? Do you think you can handle it? Getting every hole filled up and fucked?"

With a defiant gleam in my eyes, I press my ass against him. "Don't you want to find out?"

He drags his teeth across my earlobe with a single growl. As quickly as he snatched me up, he releases the grip on my neck, and though it wasn't cutting off my air, I find my chest heaving. His long strides are already carrying him through the door. I follow him into the main room, where he is standing in front of the backlit wall and selecting items that I don't get a good look at.

"Hands on the table," he says as he turns. "Bend over."

The hard edge to his voice sends chills of excitement through me. I assume the indicated position with my legs spread and my short skirt inching up my thighs. He drags the fabric the rest of the way up, exposing my ass.

I hear the click of a bottle opening, but this doesn't stop me from gasping when I feel the cold slickness of lube being drizzled across my ass. The wetness drips between my cheeks, and Hades drags his finger through the path of it, circling the tight opening.

"What are you...?" I breathe.

"Isn't this what you asked for?" he says. "Excuse me—demanded?"

My pulse ratchets higher. Admittedly, I haven't done anal before. I'm not sure what I was thinking, blustering like that. Did I really just march in there and beg to get gang banged?

"Yes, but—"

"Because I thought you said you wanted to be—"

He pushes a finger inside me, entirely ignoring the fact that this hole has never been fucked, and another desperate sound escapes my throat.

"—filled up."

"I do," I pant. "But—"

I swear as he buries himself to the knuckle, twisting his touch. Panic mingles with pleasure, because I *do* feel filled up, and I have a feeling he's planning more. Much more.

"But?" he prompts.

The admission works its way up my throat in a tight gasp. "I've never done this before."

"Relax," he instructs. "Breathe."

"Are you disappointed?" I ask. My voice is small, and I wonder if he's regretting this whole arrangement. My inexperience.

I hear the buzz of a vibrator click on. The stretching sting of his fingers contrasts the soothing pleasure of the toy against my sex. A shudder of pleasure surges through me as he rubs it up and down my slit.

"I could never be disappointed in you," he purrs. "You're my perfect horny nymph, who is so good at taking whatever I give you. Aren't you, Persephone?"

Pleasure buzzes through me.

"Yes," I breathe.

He waits for my gasps to turn to moans before he presses the toy inside my pussy, searching out my most sensitive spot. He rocks against it with expert precision. I spread my legs wider, arching back to meet his movements.

"Mmm. Do you want more?"

"Yes," I sigh.

He adds another finger to my ass. His touch slides in and out, along with the vibrator, matching my movements. Heat spreads through my body.

I have almost achieved the perfect rhythm when he removes his hand. I sigh at the sensation of going from full to gaping open. I must make some sort of noise that sounds like a protest, because I hear his smile.

"Hmm, I don't think that's enough. Maybe just a *little* more."

A little more turns out to be a *lot* more. He continues working my innermost sweet spot as he adds more lube. The second toy is cool against the curve of my backside. There's another wave of sudden, stinging pressure as he slips it inside me.

"Oh... *fuck*," I breathe. "It feels big."

I can hear him smile. "Certainly bigger than my finger."

The fullness has increased the sensation in my pussy, pressing my walls more tightly around the vibrator. I moan in response.

"Breathe," he commands.

I obey. With every breath, the sensations seem to swell, as if I'm so full that simply adding extra air in my lungs heightens the pleasure. I rock back against the toy, wondering if he's going to let me come like this.

"Is this what you wanted?"

"Yes."

"Does it make you want to come?"

"Mmhmm."

"Good," he says. "Maybe, in the future, you'll remember that my training has a purpose."

He withdraws the vibrator, clicking it off. My pussy pulses with arousal, desperate to be filled back up.

I groan out an incoherent series of vowels, smacking my palm against the table.

His laugh is an exhale. "Were those words, princess?"

"Training," I manage. "Maybe I need more of your training, sir. Before we go."

He gives my ass a playful slap, making no effort to remove the plug.

"I think you've had enough for what I've got in mind tonight. You ready?"

I cross the room toward him with my pussy wet, my heart racing, and my ass stretched around the toy. I notice the full sensation as I move, taking tentative, careful steps.

"It feels..." Big? Foreign? Like I want him to fuck my pussy until I come with this inside me?

Hades takes my hand when I reach him, gently kissing my knuckles. "Is there an adjective somewhere in that sentence?"

"It feels good," I manage with a blush. "Really good."

"Good," he grins. "Let's go."

When we stroll into the atrium, I'm desperate to get bent over the nearest sofa and pushed past the edge as quickly as possible. It should come as no surprise to me that Hades has no such urgency. He leads us to the bar, ordering a decanter of his signature rum and a couple of rocks glasses. He motions to the barstool beside him.

"Don't you want to sit?"

I'm unsure if I can sit, and the slight curve at the corner of his mouth tells me he knows this. After some careful adjusting, I manage to perch on the edge of the seat. I'm admittedly so horny I'm tempted to shimmy to see if the friction of my thighs might take the edge off. He watches this play across my face with amusement.

"Happy?" I ask, with a defiant glint in my eye.

He hides his smile in his drink. "Patience, Persephone."

My nipples go taut when he says my name like that. Like a warm, silky promise. I want to wrap it around my shoulders and slide it across my skin, between my legs.

The server returns with the requested decanter, bestowing us each with a hefty pour before replacing it on the tray.

"Would you like anything else, sir?"

"Yes, for the main course, we'll be having three—no, maybe four?" Hades glances at me as if for confirmation. "Let's go with three men, to round out the fivesome. Maybe in about half an hour. And could you reserve the pit for us?"

My brain seems to stumble over every word in this sentence, but the server never misses a beat.

"Of course, sir. Consider it done."

I chew my bottom lip, watching the server drift away and tap something into the computer.

"Fivesome," I note.

He passes my drink to me with a smirk, and I toss back a long gulp, sucking my teeth against the slight sting and wiping my mouth with the back of my hand. I'm almost scared to ask.

"What exactly am I going to do with four cocks?"

His smirk turns to a grin. "Whatever I want you to."

My whole body goes warm, like someone has poured something delicious over the top of my head and it has melted down to my toes. It's that signature blend of nervousness and excitement. I shift in my seat.

"And what exactly is 'the pit'?" I question, narrowing my gaze. "Because it sounds ominous."

"You've seen it," he says. "The terraced seating area that sinks down into the floor. It's got that ring of columns around it, and curtains, if we prefer privacy."

I remember now. The silk throw pillows. The soft, plush look to the terraced seating.

"And do we," I ask, "prefer privacy?"

"That depends. Do you want people to watch your first fivesome? Or would you like a more intimate experience?"

I smile, as if anything involving five people could be considered 'intimate.' Five people is a group. A party.

A group sex party, my brain supplies.

"I don't care if people watch," I reply after a while. "And these people aren't... I mean, they're doing this willingly, right?"

He laughs. "Yes. Nobody here has to do anything they don't want to do."

"Well," I defend with an embarrassed smile. "You ordered them off the menu like something you *own*. Or have to pay for."

"I do not own them. And honestly in this case, they would likely pay money to be in that pit with *you*, princess. It's not so wrong to think someone would pay for something they want," he says, dragging his touch up my thigh. "But no, to answer your question, there's no financial exchange here. We have an ongoing list of those looking for groups, and a schedule to reserve rooms or spaces. The director of activities and her staff keep things moving. It's all very dignified."

"Oh yes," I laugh. "So very *dignified*."

When he smiles, I can't help it. I lean in, catching his bottom lip with my teeth and drawing him into a kiss. His mouth is warm and sure and hungry. As the moment intensifies, he pulls me onto his lap, groaning when my tongue teases his. He edges my skirt higher on my hips, tapping his finger against the base of the plug, making me gasp in his mouth.

"You're going to be so much fun," he murmurs.

Four guys.

Men, really.

Well, except for the one who looks like a total college dudebro, all glory muscles and bright blue eyes and deep dimples when he smiles. He looks like he's twenty-two and ready to take full advantage of his ridiculous youth. The rest of them, though?

The guy closest to us is at least two heads taller than the dudebro, with a close cut beard and long blonde hair twisted into a bun and shaved close on the sides.

The one next to him has a broad chest, huge arms, and warm, caramelized skin, like he's been working on a boat for days on end. I realize after a beat that his body is covered in tribal tattoos, but they blend so well with the contours of his muscles that they almost seem like shadows.

The dudebro. The blonde. And the tattooed islander.

They're lounging like old friends and laughing casually when Hades sweeps the curtain open for us to step inside the space. The moment they catch sight of us, their eyes seem to widen in surprise, their jaws go slightly slack.

"Hades," the blonde says, bowing his head. "They didn't…"

"They didn't tell us it was you," the islander offers, in his smooth, deep voice. "And your queen, I presume."

"Holy shit," the dudebro whispers, as if we aren't standing right here. "That's Hades? Sick."

"I asked them not to tell you. But yes, I am in fact Hades," he says with an amused chuckle.

He takes my hand and leads me closer to the group. I smile in spite of myself as he gives me a slow spin before kissing my knuckles. "And this is Persephone."

Each of them inclines their heads. "My lady," they say in unison.

"I figured we could sort out the particulars in person," Hades offers. "Should we make ourselves comfortable?"

"Please," the blonde says with a sweep of his hand. "I'm Adonis."

"Afu," the tattooed islander offers.

The younger guy glances between all of us uncertainly before flashing his dimples. "I'm Grayson. People call me Gray. Or Son, but that might be... weird... in this scenario."

When I laugh, it seems to break some of the tension.

"We'll stick with Gray," Hades smirks.

When he takes the nearest seat, we all find ourselves draped across various levels of the terrace, pouring drinks and discussing sexual preferences, conduct guidelines, rules of engagement. It amuses me to discover that Hades wasn't exactly kidding earlier: the entire thing is very dignified.

Adonis and Afu are both wearing sarongs tied around their waists, showing off their toned torsos and strong thighs. Grayson is—unsurprisingly—naked, and wearing only a cowboy hat, which I secretly hope he'll remove at some point. But if you didn't know any better, you might think we were all a hodgepodge of friends, hanging out in a swanky VIP lounge. Except for the moment when Grayson announces that he "doesn't do butt stuff."

"Persephone is new to anal play herself," Hades says. "Want to show them, princess?"

I lick my lips with a blush, but I've had enough to drink that I climb onto my hands and knees. Hades hums approval, bending me over his thighs and slipping my skirt up over my ass to put it on display. Murmurs and smiles move through the group.

"I think we can help with that," Adonis says. He moves closer, rubbing an appreciative palm up my thigh, kissing the exposed flesh.

Hades smooths a hand up the back of Adonis's neck, fisting his bun and lifting his head. For a moment, my heart plummets and the moment stills, and I wonder if already this was a terrible, *terrible* idea. Then Hades kisses him, and the moment melts.

"I think we all can help each other," Hades purrs. "But first, let's make her comfortable."

Making me comfortable involves having me step out of my skirt and into a harness that wraps around my waist and both thighs, which snugs a nubby triangle of silicon across my clit.

"All good?" Hades asks.

I wiggle my hips a little side to side, testing it out. "I think so."

With a single click of the remote in his hand, a buzzing jolt runs through me.

"Oh!" I yelp.

My knees buckle, and I'm grateful for the plush surface beneath me when I land.

"What about now?" he says.

It's a few seconds before the vibration transitions from *oh shit no* to *holy fuck yes*. I support myself with my hands and bite into my bottom lip, but I can't stop the soft moans that escape me.

"Oh my... god."

I roll my hips as if there's someone behind me, and I *really* wish there was.

The group suddenly looks hungry, taking in every inch of my body, savoring my sounds and movements. I'm certain they're about to surround me, but as quickly as it started, the vibration stops. I murmur in protest.

"What was that, little nymph?" Hades says in that deep, teasing way of his.

I dig my knees into the cushions, spreading them wider as I wiggle my hips. "Please. Can you please turn the vibrator back on?"

"You're sure."

"Very sure," I breathe.

With one click, he has me writhing again. It feels so good—*too* good—and I grip my fingers into the velvet flooring of the pit, biting hard into my bottom lip.

Hades's voice is a deep purr. "Breathe, princess."

I do as he says, trying to ride out the sensations, but I need more. I end up writhing in the middle of the floor, reaching for the nearest pillow and squeezing it tight, but it doesn't satisfy the way I hope, especially when he inches the vibration higher.

"Fuck," I groan again. They watch as I roll onto my back, with my legs spread wide and my hands roving up my body.

"Yes, touch your tits," Hades says.

I tug them free from my top, letting my hands probe and squeeze the taut skin, pinching and pulling my nipples. It rachets up the heat between my legs, and I tip my head back with another moan, arching into the sensations. Hot shame spreads through me—or is it lust?—with the knowledge that I am touching myself in front of him. In front of *all* of them.

Hades was right: this isn't like last time. Last time I was a passive participant. This time, he's going to make me own my part in it, all these dirty fantasies I've begged for.

The men are getting hard under their sarongs, stroking themselves as they watch me. But none of them look at me like Hades: possessive, calm, in control. I know he won't let me come like this, but I lean into it anyway, teasing my nipples and rolling my hips.

Hades's voice is the dark, shadowy heat that licks through me. "Mmm. A little teasing turns you into such a perfect, slut, doesn't it, Persephone?"

A hot blush creeps up my neck when he says my name like that, but I can't stop the building pleasure. I am wet and aching.

"Yes, sir," I pant. "I'm so fucking horny."

"You want to come?"

"Yes."

"Mm. And you want us to fuck you?"

I tease my nipples with a whimper. "Please."

He clicks off the vibrator. A low growl escapes me.

When my eyes meet his, I realize what he has known all along: he only needs to tease me to turn me into this other version of myself. The regular me is blushing and demurring and all smiles. This me is feral and horny and desperate. This me feels more me than I've ever been, some pure, uninhibited version of myself. And I see that he *sees* it.

"Prove it," he says.

11

My pussy is so wet. From my current position on my hands and knees, I wonder how long until my arousal drips down my inner thighs. The dormant vibrator is still pressed against my swollen clit. My bustier is shoved down under my tits from my frantic attempt to seek pleasure before the clock ran out, and my nipples are hard and sensitive.

Hades runs his tongue between the part of his lips, beckoning me closer with a single finger.

"Crawl to us."

Us.

They all watch as I bridge the space between us, and their obvious need hits me like honeyed rum, at once warm and intoxicating. Their cocks are so hard. Adonis and Afu have already removed their sarongs so they can stroke themselves, but Grayson is watching me slack-jawed, as if he can't believe he's here, though he has finally removed his cowboy hat and is now holding it over his manhood.

Hades is, of course, still impeccably dressed. I kneel in front of him on the terrace, drawing myself between his knees and dragging my nose across his.

"What now, sir?" I breathe, my lips brushing his.

He grips my chin so I meet his gaze. "Now I want you to decide which of these cocks is going to fuck you first."

They're eagerly surrounding us. I bite my lip as I take them in. I know from before he covered it with the cowboy hat that Grayson's is shorter, but thicker. Adonis's is beautifully proportioned, with corded veins and a head that I want to suck into my mouth like a fresh peach. Afu's is just huge, like him, there's no way around it, and it may be the only part of him that isn't tattooed. It dawns on me that they're all so perfectly *fuckable*.

Some part of me is trying to decide how to choose when the vibrator clicks on. I nearly fall forward into Adonis, catching myself against his muscled thighs. As quickly as it buzzed to life, the vibration goes quiet and the ache inside me twists tighter.

"Fuck," I grit out.

"Pick one," Hades instructs. "For your pussy first. I want it nice and warmed up."

The thought of having one of them—any of them—inside me makes me feel hot and liquid, but I've never done this. Is there a right way to choose? A correct way to begin?

"I... I don't know," I stammer.

Hades snugs a finger under my chin and brings my hungry gaze to meet his again. His lips caress mine, teasing and slow.

"Let's stick to the truth, princess. I see how much you want them. Put them in your mouth first. See how they feel."

When he releases me, my eyes travel up Adonis's hard body, and he gives me an encouraging smirk. Something switches inside me. I transform from the girl who is not supposed to be so eager, who is supposed to make everything look effortless, to the girl who is greedily sliding her mouth around his cock like she *needs* it. When I flick my tongue on the underside of that beautiful head of his, Adonis curses to the faraway sky.

"Oh, fuck *yes*," he sighs.

The vibrator clicks on, almost as if it's my reward for playing nice, and I hum in satisfaction. I'm still on my knees, but I spread them wider, as if desperate for my pussy to make contact with something while Adonis is in my mouth, threading his fingers into my hair, gently pumping his hips.

After a few tantalizing moments, the vibration cuts off.

"Mm," I protest, drawing back.

"Don't get greedy," Hades says. "You've got to try them all."

Adonis is barely out of my mouth when Afu rubs the tip of his cock back and forth against my lips. I let him in with a satisfied groan, stretching my mouth around his size. I grip his thick thighs, breathe in the clean, salt-air smell of him as I try not to choke.

When the vibrator clicks on, my pleasure surges again, and I suck him harder, take him deeper until the hinge of my jaw aches. This time when the buzzing between my legs goes quiet, I release him with a few final licks.

Grayson is next, and I can tell, despite his earlier vibrato, that he's nervous. Something about this dissolves the remainder of my own anxiety. I give him a coy smile, motioning him closer with my index finger, which I suck into my mouth and run over my bottom lip.

"Can I put your cock in my mouth?" I ask, innocent and doe-eyed. "Just for a second?"

He nods, wide-eyed and wordless, before removing the cowboy hat. I take it from his hand and toss it away from us. He's harder than any of them, and he gives a full body shudder when I wrap my lips around him. I move up and down on his cock, and the rewarding vibration returns only for a few breaths. When it's time to stop, we're both panting.

From behind me, Hades gathers my hair in his hands, tugs until I'm looking up at him.

"So," he says. "Who's it going to be fucking you first?"

"Adonis," I say.

Hades's eyes flicker with feral delight, and he releases me.

"As you wish."

This is all the permission Adonis needs. His intense gaze rakes my body as he comes to his knees, prowling toward me. His hand slides up my throat, over the collar, until my mouth meets his.

"I want to know," he says against my lips. "Is your pussy as sweet and wet as your mouth?"

Suddenly, one of his strong arms wraps around me and he's pressing me back into the soft embrace of the pillows on the floor. His cock fits into me like a lock sliding closed, feeling so tight inside me against the pressure of the anal plug.

"Oh!" I sigh.

It would feel wrong to be this close to him—to be getting *fucked* by him—except that Hades is kneeling overhead, giving me upside-down kisses. My mouth meets his greedily, somehow hoping the familiarity of his touch will ground me as all the new sensations threaten to sweep me away.

Hades motions Grayson closer and guides him to his knees above my head.

"Suck his cock for me, princess," Hades says. I open my mouth like a hungry baby bird, loving the feel of my tongue sliding over the contours of Grayson as he sighs out garbled words.

When Hades's next coaxing words come, I can't tell if it's me or Gray that he's encouraging.

"That's it," he purrs. "Just like that."

Without being told, Afu positions himself behind Adonis, who stills inside me as the other man enters him. With a few testing thrusts, their rhythm syncs, and Adonis gets harder inside me, as if getting fucked while he fucks me is his ultimate turn-on.

"You like that, pretty boy?" Afu growls.

"Yes," Adonis groans. "Fuck yes."

It's the same chorus that is resounding in my own head, while I watch Afu's giant hands wrap around Adonis's lean abs as he thrusts into him. Each beat of their rhythm sends Adonis harder into me.

"Dude," Grayson interrupts. "You guys are way too into this."

Adonis gives Gray a scandalous smile before reaching forward and grabbing him by the back of the neck, claiming his mouth with his. I want to laugh at how I feel Grayson's cock pulse as he softens into the kiss. I flick my tongue across him, reveling in the teasing as he loses his breath. Adonis's other hand drags one of my knees over his shoulder so he can take me deeper.

Hades watches all of this, taking a slow sip of his drink as he undresses in that unhurried way: unbuttoning his shirt, unzipping his pants, letting everything fall soundlessly to the floor. His cock is so hard, and even though I'm filled up, it's him that I want in every part of me.

Almost as if he can sense this thought, he clicks the vibrator on again—my own little reward. I groan loudly around Grayson's girth.

Oh yes. *Fuck. Yes.*

As I edge closer to absolute oblivion, I expect Hades to deny me at any second, but he keeps the vibration going as he draws closer, dragging his fingers across my chest, circling my nipples. He drops to his knees to suck one between his lips, tugging it between his teeth.

I release Grayson's cock with a moan.

"Oh my *god.*"

"Right here, princess," Hades says, flicking his tongue up and down the sensitive rosebud flesh. "Be a good little slut and put his cock back in your mouth."

I do as he says, and he continues to play with my tits, clicking the vibration higher with the small remote in his hand. My legs are wide open now, with Adonis pumping into me, and Afu biting his shoulder, and I've never been so delirious with pleasure. I'm desperate to hold onto it. The past few days have taught me that Hades loves to tease and taunt me, always pulling back when I'm right at the edge, and if he does that right now, I may break.

By some miracle, the ecstasy continues. The toy in my ass is sending Adonis into exactly the right spot as Hades flicks his tongue across my hard nipple. Up and down, up and down. I remove Grayson from my mouth again.

"I'm going to come," I pant.

Hades tugs my nipple between his teeth, pinching the other tightly. "I'll let you come—if you put that cock back in your mouth."

The thing about the cock in my mouth is that it doesn't have much longer, and I know it. Grayson's breaths are coming hard and fast, and his balls have gone taut, and he's going to explode at any time. I don't care. I suck harder, letting it drive me to the edge with a fervent groan.

Hades continues to tease my tits. "Don't you dare stop sucking that cock, Persephone. I want you completely filled up when you come. Your mouth. Your pussy. Your ass."

Oh god.

I'm close. So close I can feel my pleasure like a cresting wave. So close that the loud, moaning sounds I'm making around Grayson's cock almost seem faraway, because all I can think is *yes, yes, fuck*—

I am swept under. My orgasm comes in hot, helpless layers: my pussy clenching around Adonis, my clit throbbing against the toy, my ass pulsing around the plug, and the sound of my moans muffled by Grayson, who is already pulling out and spilling hot cum across my tits.

"Oh my god." I gasp as I attempt to ride out the orgasm, but it never seems to end. "Oh my god I can't—stop."

Adonis takes my climax as a signal to pull out. After a few sensual thrusts, Afu does the same. Hades, however, lingers.

"Please... stop... I'm—"

I'm almost convulsing when he finally clicks off the vibrator. My entire body goes limp against the embrace of the soft velvet floor.

"Did you come for us, princess?" he teases.

He leans forward to lick the cum off my tits, which he sucks and bites, spreading the sticky-hot liquid across me like icing on a pair of plump cinnamon rolls. Every touch jolts through me.

"Yes," I whimper.

I'm still oversensitive when Hades drags me on top of him.

"Mmm. Come here. I want to feel you."

It feels so good to bury him inside me that every nerve in my body seems to sigh with relief. I tip my head back, smoothing my hands through my hair with a long exhale.

"Fuck you're hard," I breathe.

"And you're so very wet," he says, circling his fingers around the point where we're connected, feeling my stretched opening. "Almost like you like getting passed around and fucked by all of us. Like it turns you on."

"It does," I admit. "I'm so fucking horny."

"I thought you just came," he taunts.

I give him an impish pout. "I want to come more."

He meets the rhythm of my hips with eager thrusts. "How are you so fucking perfect?"

For a few glorious moments, he lets me ride his cock, until Adonis and Afu return, summoned by this new position. Neither of them have finished yet, and they're eager to join us.

"Take the toy out of her ass," Hades says. "She needs to get fucked."

"With pleasure," Afu grins.

With Hades still inside me, I feel Afu's hands on my hips, tipping me forward onto my hands and knees, caressing the curve of my backside. Then he drags his thick fingers between my cheeks to remove the toy, and—

"*Oh!*" I gasp.

After hours of getting used to a sensation of fullness, I now feel gaping open. The cool slickness of lube spreads as Afu inserts a finger, which I'm relieved to find feels nothing like it did earlier. I take his testing strokes easily.

"Such a tight little ass," he hums.

"A virgin ass," Hades says. His eyes are locked on mine, and I hold onto his gaze like a lifeline. "You'll have to play nice."

"We're always nice," Afu smirks. I gasp a little as he inserts another thick finger, still surprised at the comfortable feel of it.

Meanwhile, Adonis has knelt right in front of me, with his glistening cock eager. Hades guides him into my mouth, inches above his face.

"Mmm," I moan.

Hades strokes my tits encouragingly as Afu adds a third finger, and all I can think is *more*. How I could possibly still crave anything more seems delusional, and yet, I want it all. I want to get fucked by all three of these men at once.

Despite this, when Afu attempts to stuff the entirety of his giant cock into my ass, I release Adonis from my mouth with a sharp cry.

"Holy fuck. Wait."

Adonis smooths a reassuring hand through my hair. "You have to breathe."

"It's too big," I pant.

"Didn't you say you wanted to take all these cocks?" Hades argues. "Wanted us to fill you up? Every hole?"

"Yes, but—"

Suddenly, the vibrator I've almost forgotten about clicks on. I whimper.

"Yes, but what?" Hades says, his tone as hard as the length of him inside me.

I can't think with the toy buzzing against my swollen clit. I only manage to furrow my brow through a garbled groan and dig my fingernails into Hades's firm chest.

"If you don't breathe and tell us how much you want us to fuck you, Persephone, I swear I'll stop everything right now and punish your ass until you can't sit down for a week," he growls.

"No! Please," I gasp. "Please, I don't want to stop."

"And?" he prompts.

My head is spinning. I am equal parts desperation, anticipation, and lust. It's a combination that leaves me grinding against Hades. Everything inside me feels coiled tight.

"And I want to get fucked. Everywhere. Please."

Hades grins as he threads his hands over the top of mine, where I'm clawing into him so tightly that when I release him his skin will be marked with small half moons.

"Good girl," he breathes.

The praise combined with the vibrator makes me want to melt. I bury Hades all the way inside me, stilling as Afu's large hands frame my hips, making reassuring strokes across my low back. He enters me again. Another inch, and I whimper.

"Relax," Hades says. "And then it'll feel so very good. Ask Adonis."

Adonis strokes my hair again, giving me a wink when my questioning gaze flits up to his. "Promise."

I take a shuddering breath, and all at once my body yields. Hades's eyes go blown-out and black, and the knowledge that we're sharing this sensation of Afu's cock sliding into me is almost as intense as the physical feeling of being so, fucking, full.

Hades. Afu. Both of them inside of me, stretching me, filling me.

When Afu reaches his hilt, he groans as if he's just slipped into the hot embrace of one of the palace pools filled by the river Styx.

"Fucking perfect," he sighs, as he spreads his hands wide over my hips.

Beneath me, Hades kisses my wrist. "Your move, princess. Fuck us however you want. Make yourself feel good."

I take a tentative shift, sucking in a breath at the subtle sting. But then, after the next few movements, I realize it *does* feel good. So, fucking, good.

"I..."

I quickly lose my train of thought, along with my breath. I become only pleasure, warm and liquid and gasping as I move against them. Sliding in and out slowly. Reveling in their sensual sighs when I sink all the way back down.

"Oh, fuck yes," Hades groans. "You are a fucking goddess, Persephone."

He watches me with ferocious intensity as I fuck them both. I take Adonis back into my mouth, and he laughs with surprise as my lips wrap around him, threading his hand into my hair again.

"Yeah, you got it, baby," he sighs.

"She's so fucking tight," Afu groans.

He's meeting the little thrusts of my hips with restraint. I can tell he wants to pound into me, but he lets me take my pleasure from them, and I am vibrating with it.

"Come here," Afu says, somewhere over his shoulder. "Fuck, you have to feel this."

Suddenly Afu slides out. I feel the weight of his cock against the curve of my ass as he guides Grayson into his place. The trade-off leaves me moaning, as if for a terrifying moment they're going to accidentally attempt to take me at the same time. I feel Afu stroking himself as Gray sinks all the way inside me.

"Oh, holy shit," he groans.

I shift back against Gray with slow, tentative movements, but almost immediately, he gets overzealous. I cry out from the sudden sting of his thrusts, which results in a smacking sound as Afu knocks him on the shoulder.

"Ow!" Gray protests. "What was that for."

I let out another gasping cry as Afu shoves Gray away from me. "I said feel it, you idiot, not make her scream."

In another instant, I feel Afu sliding himself up and down over my gaping entrance. He puts a protective hand on the curve of my backside, palming my hip.

"Do you need us to stop, my lady?" he asks.

I sink against Hades, who licks encouragingly at my breasts. Pleasure rushes in to soothe the pain.

"Is that all you can take?" he teases, sucking one of my nipples into his mouth. "You want us to stop?"

"No," I breathe. "Please don't stop."

Adonis grins, guiding my lips back around him. "You have the most exquisite mouth," he says, stroking my jaw. "Your pussy, too. But the way you suck me off makes me want to come all over your pretty face."

I moan in an eager response, taking him deeper. Almost as a reward, the intensity of the vibrator edges higher. Afu takes this opportunity to insert himself again, and my eyes roll closed in absolute surrender.

"That's it," Hades coaxes, kissing my neck. "Take all these fucking cocks, princess. Show me how much you want to come for us."

He knows I'm close. His pupils are like black pools in a deep ocean as I ride him, while Afu fucks my ass and Adonis fucks my mouth. Beads of sweat—or maybe hot tears—slide down my face, and I move against them faster, because nothing has ever felt this good.

"Oh my god," I gasp.

Adonis's cock slips in and out of my open mouth, and he's stroking himself hard and fast, chasing his own release. With a garbled groan, Afu also withdraws, leaving me empty and gasping as he spills hot cum all over my ass. It pools in the curve of my low back, drips down my thighs.

Adonis is quick to follow, with his release spilling down my chin, across my breasts, and onto Hades's chest.

My climax racks my entire body. The vibration is suddenly too much, but it doesn't stop. I scream at the pleasure, which seems to have no end. I find myself riding out what is possibly another orgasm or a cresting wave of the first. My pussy throbs around Hades.

"I can't stop," I cry. "Please... stop. Stop!"

"You're so beautiful when you beg," Hades growls, fucking me harder.

For days, he's been holding me at the edge. Now, he won't let up. I'm almost convinced, as my eyes roll closed, that I'm going to black out. I cease to be flesh and bones, and I am only ether, as infinite as the night sky, burning like the stars.

Finally, mercifully, the vibrator goes quiet. I suck in deep, gasping breaths as I attempt to resurface.

"You're trying... to kill me?" I murmur.

"Quite the opposite. I'm trying to make you feel alive."

Hades draws my mouth against his, kissing me deeply as he reverses our positions. In one smooth motion, he rolls me onto my back so he can hook my thigh around his torso and thrust into me deeply. I meet his open mouth with a moan.

"Do you have any idea how hot it is watching you get fucked?" he asks. "You take those cocks so, fucking, well."

He caresses my bottom lip, and I tease his tongue, and suddenly we're licking and sucking the salty sweetness off of each other while he buries himself inside me again, and again, and again.

"Oh my god, you feel so good," I whimper. And he does. Everyone feels different, but he feels so *right*.

"You like being mine?" he says.

"I love being yours. I love..."

His gaze locks into mine, and he hits just the right spot, and I cry out again.

"Fuck, I love you," I moan.

His eyes have gone wide, but any reply he might offer is lost to the force of his release, and my face burns with what I've said. Every part of my brain that isn't numb with pleasure scrambles, wondering if there's any way to take it back, but my chest swells with certainty because... it's the truth, isn't it?

It's only when we're both completely unraveled and struggling for air, that I realize there are tears rolling down my face.

Not just tears. I'm crying. My chest is rising and falling with hiccupping breaths. Full body sobs rack me.

Panic and confusion have twisted Hades's features. He quickly scoops me into his arms, holding me against his chest while the other guys rush up the terrace to close the curtains tightly against onlookers, grab me a towel, fetch me a glass of water.

"Shh," Hades soothes, holding me tight. "What's the matter?"

"My lady, did we hurt you?" Afu asks.

"I didn't mean to!" Grayson pipes up, eager to set the record straight. Someone shushes him with a warning swat to the shoulder.

I press my hot, sticky, tear-streaked face into Hades's chest, embarrassed. "No. No. I'm sorry. I'm so—"

"Don't apologize," Hades murmurs against my hair. "You didn't do anything wrong."

Does that mean I didn't *say* anything wrong, either? I'm terrified to know, and I'm desperate to explain this away.

"I've just never felt so... much. Too much."

Adonis lifts my face and gives me a reassuring smile, using a cool towel to wipe my hot cheeks. "The first time is always a lot. And Afu especially is a lot. Too much, probably. Trust me on this."

Afu grins, elbowing him, and they laugh, sharing a brief, playful kiss.

When I exhale a weak laugh, some of the tension in my chest lessens. "It was good. I'm fine. I..."

Grayson passes me a glass of rum. "Seriously? You were amazing. You made that look easy. All I did was come too quick like an idiot."

They all laugh again.

I bite my bottom lip with a nod of thanks, but I realize the tears are still coming. Hades thumbs away the wetness and draws my gaze back to his. Concern has furrowed his dark brow but softened his eyes. When I breathe in again, I'm enveloped by the warm, comforting smell of him, and suddenly, it's as if there are only the two of us.

"Persephone," he says, pressing his forehead against mine.

My voice is barely a whisper. "Yes?"

"I love you, too."

My eyes well again, and I snag my lip with my teeth. I give him a questioning nod, as if to say, *You do?*

His gaze dances across my face, soft and serious, and his mouth quirks at one corner, sweet and kissable.

Yes, my nymph, my princess, my queen, *I do.*

The accepted custom is to occupy the pit while recovering, which is more than welcome, because I'm too pleasure-drunk to move even if I wanted to. I gulp down cool water for my raw throat, allow Hades to peel off my ruined thigh-high tights, drape me in a fresh pashmina, and settle me into a nest of silk pillows. He tucks himself protectively beside me, sweeping my sweaty hair away from my face. Adonis lounges on my other side, quietly braiding the messy length of it. Grayson sucks down complimentary beverages while watching him and asking questions. And Afu returns with a small cylinder of salve that smells like peppermint and eucalyptus.

"For your backside," he explains, shrugging the container in his large hand. "May I?"

I blink, trying to understand if he's actually asking if he can touch my ass in a non-sexual way after he fucked the hell out of it. My mouth opens, then hangs ajar, because I'm not sure how to answer a question like this.

"Take some," Hades insists. "You'll thank him later."

"Yes, Your Highness," Adonis laughs, patting the side of his own bare butt. "Trust him on this."

My eyes slide closed as I laugh, embarrassed about being embarrassed.

I carefully roll onto my belly, allowing Hades to stroke the sensitive nape of my neck while Afu tenderly applies the ointment. Immediately, I go from feeling slightly wrecked to tingly and cool. I glance over my shoulder to where Adonis is finishing up his handiwork with my hair.

"You don't have to call me that, you know," I tell him, catching the curious flash of his green eyes. "'Your Highness', I mean. I'm just Persephone."

"Just Persephone," he teases. "Or, Persephone the Just. A fitting name for a queen."

I give him a good-natured roll of my eyes.

"You know," he continues, finally tying off the end of my braid with the band he removed from his own hair. Its golden length falls around his strong shoulders. "I heard what you did. Letting Orpheus cross over to try and find his wife. For someone who says she isn't a queen, that's a lot of power you hold."

I only have to search his gaze for a moment to land on the truth behind his words. Adonis is already moving away, settling into his own nest of pillows and allowing Afu to pour him a drink. Immediately, I turn to Hades.

"You let the lovesick musician go to the Underworld?" I say, wide-eyed and wondering. "And he lived?"

"The Fates have yet to say if he should live or die. But yes, I let him go. Or should I say *you* let him go, in your first unofficial act as queen."

I bite my bottom lip, letting my gaze study the face of this man who perpetually surprises me. His features—that are often mistaken as bored or disappointed—have such a flickering depth that the overall effect is like dipping myself into a pool and realizing with surprise that I can't reach the bottom.

He reaches up and smooths the furrow between my brows. "I thought you'd be happy."

"I am happy," I admit, grasping his hand and kissing it. "So happy it hurts."

"I never mean to hurt you, Persephone. You know that, don't you? These games..."

"I love the games we play," I admit.

My body is still thrumming with the pleasure of it, in a way I can't ignore, but my next words are shy.

"I would understand if that's all it is for you. What you really meant, when you said you loved me – that you just, ya know, love the way we fuck. I mean, the sex is unthinkably amazing."

He threads his fingers through mine, and I can't tell if it's for reassurance or consolation. My chest clenches.

"I'd be lying if I said I don't love seeing you like you were earlier, on your knees, completely ravenous, begging for more. But I meant it when I said I love you. I'm not sure I can separate the two, because the same woman who captured my heart is the one I want in my bed. Why can't it be both?"

My heart is thick in my throat. I swallow.

"It can be both. Maybe it is both."

One corner of his mouth twitches, and he nods again.

"The best of both worlds."

As I snuggle against him again, I wonder which 'worlds' he means. My world? The Underworld? I'm torn between kissing his chest and peppering him with more questions, when the high notes of a playful argument rise up from the pillows beside us.

"C'mon!" Grayson says, reaching for the small container in Afu's hand while Adonis wrestles him away. "You guys are being dicks."

"This isn't for you," Afu says, holding it just out of Gray's reach as he paws the air. "You can't use the salve unless you do 'butt stuff.'"

Adonis laughs as Grayson shifts into an angry pout.

"Fine," he harrumphs, pointing to Adonis, then to Afu. "But I want the smaller one. Keep your monster dick away from me."

I sink back into the pillows with a chortle. "Should we leave them to fight it out?"

Hades smirks. "Are you saying you've had enough?"

I give him a coy look. "For now."

We gather ourselves up while the trio is still arguing over semantics and bid them goodbye as if they're friends of friends we ran into at a bar and not men we fucked. Hades snags a decanter of rum as we slip through the curtains and back into the noise of the atrium. After a quick shortcut hidden between towering palms, we're back in the privacy of our passageways, stumbling barefoot across the limestone and taking giddy swigs straight from the bottle as we make our way to the bath.

12

Late summer turns into early fall with a cool sigh of relief, the way it often does. I smell it on the breezes that come off the river, though the cold never quite reaches us here in the palace. The floors stay slightly warm under my bare feet. The leaves don't turn those signature shades of red or gold. The days don't get shorter. But the next time Juno sweeps into the palace unannounced, she's wearing a fashionable sweater, scarf, and boots combo, looking every bit like she stepped out of a cozy fall mood board.

We're still in bed when she arrives, and this time I don't scramble to cover myself. Hades groans, hooking an arm over his eyes.

"Could you start waiting until we've had breakfast before you barge in unannounced?"

She tosses her phone on the bed between us. "You'll want to see this."

I cautiously pick it up. A video is paused on the screen from Olympic Broadcast News. I recognize it as one of the premier information outlets across the river, but not one I frequent; it's usually preferred by older generations who still prefer the classic TV anchor format.

Juno raises her eyebrows as if saying, *Go ahead. Press play.*

I wait for Hades to groan himself upright before I do. His body is warm beside mine as we hover over the screen.

"We've received insider reports that Persephone Bauer, the daughter of Demeter Bauer and heiress of the Big Farma fortune, is currently being held against her will across the river Styx. The family is calling for her immediate release."

"Oh my god," I gasp. "What is—"

Suddenly, my mom is on the screen. Her swoop of short, white-blonde hair is perfectly coiffed. Her chin and nose come to dignified points, and her mouth is tight, with thin lines around it. She has never in my memory turned on the water works for the camera, but she does it now as if she's Meryl Streep preparing to collect her next Oscar.

"Many of you know me as a businesswoman, but first and foremost, I am a mother. I'm sure any parents among us can sympathize that I am desperate to have her home safe. I appreciate your support during this very difficult time."

She punches those last three words for emphasis.

Very.

Difficult.

Time.

"What difficult time?" I rant, as if demanding an answer from the screen. "She barely even saw me when I was home unless she needed me to *attend* something, and—"

The video switches back to the news anchor.

"Demeter has promised a sizable cash reward to anyone that provides information on the exact whereabouts of Persephone or her apparent captor, Hades, that assists with her rescue."

"Apparent captor! Rescue?!" I screech. "This is outrageous! You didn't kidnap me!"

Hades plucks the phone from my hand and returns it to Juno before dragging a hand across his face.

"I know," he sighs.

"Well, what are we going to do?" I demand.

He glares at Juno. "Any advice, dear sister?"

A spark of hope flares within me. "Yes! Isn't this your area of expertise? Families, or whatever?"

Juno has already perched on the edge of an armchair and is sipping coffee from a to-go mug that she hugs with both hands.

"Families are complicated," she says, non-committal.

I scrunch my face in exasperation, and before I can protest further, Hades kisses my temple.

"Coffee?" he whispers against my ear. I soften into his touch.

"Yes, please," I murmur, defeated.

He climbs out of bed and grabs a sarong from the floor, knotting it at his waist as he crosses toward the steaming carafe of dark roast that is waiting for us every morning.

"Is this why you came by?" he asks Juno. "To drop this lovely bit of news in our bed like a bomb and refuse to help clean up the mess? I'd expect this from Hermes, but not from you."

"Somebody had to tell you," she shrugs. "And I figured it might as well be someone you like."

"Speaking of Hermes, what's HMZ saying about this?"

"Nothing. Yet."

The coffee glugs as he pours two cups, adjusting mine with the appropriate amounts of cream and sugar. The clink of the spoon fills the silence. He passes me my cup while I still sit in bed, unable to move. I attempt to allow the first sip to bring me back to baseline, but it doesn't hit quite the way I hoped. None of this makes sense. I've gotten so comfortable here.

Too comfortable, I guess.

I sigh again. "She can't..."

I can't finish the sentence, because I know very well that whatever it is, my mother in fact *can*. She can lie to the press. She can make outrageous demands. She can pay off reporters, and lobbyists, and lawmakers. She's been doing it my whole life. It was easier to ignore when I was playing by her rules.

My heart flails in my chest.

"What else are they saying?" Hades asks.

"The usual. You're kidnapping women, making them sell their souls, blah blah blah."

He nods as if she's just spouted off items from her grocery list.

"I'll let Charon know to be vigilant and have the guards triple the canine patrols." He lays a reassuring hand on my shoulder. "I doubt they'd be stupid enough to try to send anyone to abduct you."

"Probably not," Juno supplies. "But what else will Demeter cook up in the meantime?"

Abduction, it seems, is the least of my worries, which is not a comforting thought.

I think about the funding for my company, but I've been checking the books obsessively each morning and night, and thus far everything has been business as usual. Up until now, most of my coworkers have believed I'm frolicking with a new boyfriend around Europe or lounging on some exotic coast—which is basically true if you substitute 'Europe' for 'Hades's palace' and 'exotic coast' for 'the bluffs of the river Styx.'

I wonder what they'll all say now.

"I mean," I say, thinking aloud. "I could go online, same as her. Tell everyone it's all a bunch of lies. Tell them the truth."

Hades shakes his head. "She's baiting you."

"Well, I have to do something! I can't just sit here and let her say these things about me. About you. Us!"

Juno holds up a hand. "He has a point. You've tried to set a boundary with her, and now she's pushing it. Sometimes the thing to do in these cases is to hold your ground. This is your life. These are your choices."

I scowl into my coffee. "Yes, but—"

Juno holds up a hand. "Please don't tell me you're about to argue that you aren't entitled to these things."

Oh god, I think. *Was I?*

"No," I say. "Of course not."

"If she's used to you jumping when she says jump, maybe this time you sit. And calmly explain to her that you're an autonomous adult who can choose to sit if she wants to. Metaphorically speaking."

I puff out my cheeks with a deflated sigh. "There is nothing calm about talking to my mother."

"Give her a call. What can it hurt?"

"My pride," I grumble into my mug.

When Juno laughs, even Hades cracks a smile.

"Maybe we should have breakfast out," he suggests. "Take a walk. Get some air. Sometimes decisions like this need room to breathe."

We get dressed—me in a breezy button-down and comfy jeans and Hades in dark khakis and a crisp white shirt, a distinct change from his usual all-black ensembles, as if he's quite literally trying to lighten the mood.

The narrow, winding paths lead us through the terraced village as a trio, and we settle onto the patio of my favorite cafe with morning sun soft on our shoulders and people bustling by, going about their daily activities. There are so many things to love about this spot, like the overflowing planters of peonies that edge the space or the fact that it's frequented by an oversized orange cat that does figure eights between my ankles before lazing in the window. At this time of day it's delightfully sunny, perfect for the wide brim boater hat I usually wear for gardening. There's a wooden wagon full of paperbacks near the door, for when I'm feeling in the mood for good company.

Usually, I revel in how picturesquely normal it all feels. But today, as we're served tiny cups of espresso and spanakopita, while the old couple inside carries on the same comically spirited argument they've been having every day since I've been coming here—the same one they've probably been having every day for the past fifty years, truth be told—the normalcy rankles. I find myself tipping my head down, studying the menu I know by heart as an excuse to hide beneath the brim of my hat.

I doubt anyone watches Olympic Broadcast News here. Why would they? In the same way no one here has ever cared to ask who my parents are or—as often happens back home—has whispered enough to already know. For weeks, I've been deriving such power from this anonymity, as if it's a kind of freedom, but suddenly, I feel like I'm mentally fighting a battle that no one knows anything about. And it feels *weird*. To simultaneously be so known and yet not known at all.

"Persephone."

Hades's voice brings me back. My breakfast sits in front of me, mostly untouched. Juno is looking at me like she's awaiting a response to a question I didn't hear.

A sweet breeze tousles my hair, and I force a smile.

"Sorry. What were you saying?"

"I was asking if you have plans later. There's a great pottery not too far from here, and I always like to stop in while I'm on this side of the river. Have you ever tried your hand at it? I'm terrible at working with clay, but it's kind of meditative. Soothing. You're welcome to join me if you like."

I catch myself in the middle of a rote response. It's been hard to break the habit, after so many years playing the agreeable daughter, but after a few stammering starts, I manage to summon something genuine.

"Thank you. Another time, maybe? My head is all over the place, and I think I need to be alone with my thoughts for a while."

She inclines her head. "Understood. Maybe I'll drag this guy with me. It's been too long since he's been behind the wheel."

The image of Hades sitting at a pottery wheel draws a smile out of me.

"You make... pottery," I note.

"Not well," he offers.

I raise an eyebrow. "I'm surprised that you say it isn't good, because I happen to know you're very good with your hands."

He accepts my teasing with a purr and tips my hat back until his nose brushes mine. "Maybe I save it all for you, princess."

"Hm," I murmur. "I guess we'll find out later, won't we?"

He reaches under the table and slides a hand up my thigh, squeezing playfully. "Who says we have to wait until later?"

I lean into his smile. When our lips touch, I feel present. It's fleeting, but it's there, tucked between these short, sweet kisses. I snag his bottom lip with my teeth, hoping to hold onto it a moment longer.

Juno clears her throat, unimpressed with our public displays, and we each settle back into our respective seats like chastised children. Hades accentuates his words in a way that lets her know she now has our full attention.

"It seems," he says, giving her an annoyed smile, "that we all have a full morning, then."

My morning is admittedly fuller than I'd like. Full of anxiety, and worry, and snippets of the news clip stuck on a permanent loop.

After breakfast, I wander off on my own and find myself in one of the many terraced gardens around the palace. I say hello to the usual gardeners and grab my gloves from a basket in the shed. It shouldn't surprise me that my feet led me here, as they do so often after breakfast. It's been part of my life for so long now, starting my mornings tending to growing things, that when nothing else makes sense, I long to have my hands in the earth.

The weeks I've been here are stacking up, and in that time I've become acquainted with the things that grow on this side of the river. As I suspected my first night here, these aren't my mother's strains and seeds. These plants have been allowed to flower and bear fruit in an unapologetic way that owes nothing to no one. Each time I uproot a carrot or pluck a zucchini from the vine, I marvel at the difference compared to the produce I've gotten used to—especially the kind we're being allowed to grow among the gardens of Bounty's small operation, under her control.

I wonder as I fill my basket if I'm the same, if in her world I had grown smaller to keep her happy, only to come here and flourish.

I should call her.

I drive my spade into the ground and wipe my dirty hand on my jeans, before fishing my phone out of my pocket. I haven't used it for much up to this point, but I take it out of airplane mode (which I've taken to referring to as 'Underworld mode') and scroll to her contact. She answers on the fifth ring, half a breath before I'm considering hanging up.

So much for the image of her waiting by the phone.

"I take it you've seen the news," she says coolly.

"Please stop this," I say. "I'm not coming home because you demanded it on live television. This is extortion."

"Well," she offers, without a hint of the sobbing woman I saw on the news. "It's worked just fine for centuries."

Anger flares, and I grit my teeth, but I refuse to let her know she's gotten a rise out of me. I close my eyes and take a slow, steady sip of morning through my nose.

"This is my life. These are my choices. I'm asking you to respect that. I'm happy here."

"Hm." I can hear her smug smile, and I hate it. "I dare say you won't be for much longer."

"Why do you care?" I demand. "Where I live. What I do. Why do you care so much?"

"You're my *daughter*." She emphasizes it so dramatically that it sounds disingenuous. "But you're young, and you don't yet have children, so I don't expect you to understand."

I roll my eyes to the thin layer of gray clouds creeping across the river, hinting of afternoon rain.

"What I don't understand is why I can't still be your daughter from here."

As I say it, though, I know why. Demeter's daughter is supposed to show up to corporate events to smile and schmooze and promote the "Big Farma: feeding our family and yours" image. She's supposed to run the offshoot of the company that improves PR ratings. She's supposed to date guys from equally powerful families—bonus points if they've got strong political ties—and probably marry one of them.

She's not supposed to run off across the river and get voluntarily stripped naked, flogged, and fucked on the altar of Hades. She's not supposed to call herself Queen of the Underworld. And she's certainly not supposed to say 'no' to the woman who conducts herself as if she's the god of all growing things, as if she's Mother Earth herself.

Her reply cuts like a freshly whetted scythe. "Let me know when you're ready to come home."

The call disconnects.

13

I run the conversation over in my head so many times that if it were a stone all of its edges would have been rubbed smooth. I attempt to work out my frustration with my knees in the dirt, pulling weeds by hand until my palms ache. With every tug I imagine that I could pluck the angry thoughts of her from my mind like these rogue shoots, but in truth it barely takes the edge off.

When the sun slips behind clouds and the breeze begins to threaten rain, the rest of the crew takes a sign from the weather to finish up for the day. I almost think about joining them, but the idea of sitting still makes me feel antsy. So instead of seeking shelter, I stubbornly commit myself to the task of propagating pomegranate cuttings from the orchard and considering ways to smuggle seeds across the river.

"I thought I might find you here," Hades says. "You seem to think better when you've got dirt under your fingernails."

I study my hands with a half-hearted smile before letting them fall to my side. It's only with Hades silhouetted in front of the backdrop of dark, grumbling clouds that I wonder how long I've been here. A gust of wind sweeps his hair across his forehead.

"She's not planning to stop," I tell him.

I've been grappling with this fact ever since the ill-advised call with my mother. How could I possibly be related to someone like her? How could we be the same?

"Did you really expect her to?" he asks gently.

I want to say yes, but I know it's not the truth. Eventually, I give a frustrated shrug.

His nod is sympathetic, but his tone is resigned. "You know you could go home if you want."

My gaze snaps to his, and at once I'm confused, and hurt, and angry all over again. "Why would I want that?"

"I'm not saying you do."

I drive my spade into the nearest pot of soil. "Then what are you saying?"

"I'm saying you're a young, vibrant woman with every opportunity ahead of her."

"And?" I demand.

"And women like you want marriage—"

"Then marry me."

"—and children. If you stay with me, you'll never be a mother."

I cross my arms over my chest, seething.

"Who said I want to be a mother?"

"I haven't heard you say you don't."

"So, you think I'm, what, 'hysterical', then? Suffering from a 'wandering womb' that will slowly drive me crazy unless it's filled up with babies? Is that it?"

"No," he says evenly. "I was not diagnosing you with any make-believe medical conditions. I was stating a fact."

A fact, I scoff.

"Why are you doing this?" I demand. "Today, of all days, you want to argue with me about procreating?!"

"I want you to think this through. I want you to know what you're giving up if you stay here."

"What I'm giving up? A life that felt suffocating? A mother who only ever used me as a political pawn—who is *still* using me, by the way—and friends who haven't bothered to call for anything other than happy hour until they saw me on the news?"

He levels his gaze.

"Your *future*."

"Not every future has to have kids," I argue. "What we have is important. I don't need a baby to validate me. To validate us!"

"*Persephone.*"

My name is a low growl. A warning. And he's obviously lost his damn mind if he thinks I'm going to heed it.

"*Why* aren't you listening to me?" I challenge. "Why is no one listening to me today? It's like when the gods gave me a uterus, it ensured I don't speak at a register that can be heard by people with power!"

At this, Hades stalks towards me. He slips his hand up the back of my neck and tips my mouth towards his, holding me mere millimeters out of reach. I gasp a little—at the sudden closeness, the tightness of his hand in my hair, the intensity of his eyes, locking with mine. My startled moan falls across his lips.

"I am listening." It's only when his voice is lethally quiet that I realize I've been yelling. "What is it that you want?"

My nostrils flare, and I huff. "What I *want* is for everyone to stop telling me what I want."

"Mmm. And here I thought you liked to be told what to do."

I'm suddenly so aware of the presence of him. All day I've been trapped in my head, spinning in circles, but when he looks at me like this, I am only here, with my shoes in the dirt, rain prickling my face, and my pulse flickering in my throat. My voice, when I find it, is a sultry hum.

"You're trying to distract me from the fact I'm angry, and it pisses me off."

His mouth gives the slightest lift at the corner, but he twists my hair around his hand until I whimper at the tightness.

"I like you angry. Anger is after all, a kind of passion, isn't it? Your heart, pounding. Your energy, electric. Your focus so, very, *tight*."

This twists through me.

"And you can't decide," he continues slowly, "if you want to kill me or fuck me. So, princess, which is it?"

He licks the parted crease of my mouth, and I shudder a sigh. I kiss him hard, the way I know will leave my lips swollen later, and I don't care. I drag my dirty hands up the front of his clean white shirt and bite his bottom lip until he groans out curses.

I'm not sure what I'm doing. We never have sex in the village, and it's clear from the way I feel him getting hard against my thigh that things are quickly heading in that direction. When he scoops me up and hooks my legs around his waist, I expect him to march me straight to bed.

But the rain is picking up. What started as a spitting mist has escalated to a steady shower that wets our clothes in big, relentless blotches. I break our kiss so I can tuck my face against his chest, trying to fend off the sudden downpour. Thunder cracks ominously, vibrating right down to my bones.

In a few quick strides, he moves us under the open edge of the garden shed, setting me on the nearest workbench. Inside, torrents of rain cascade off the roof, enveloping us as if we're tucked behind a waterfall. For a few moments, we let the present catch up to us. Our chests heaving. Our hair in dark, damp tendrils. The dusty smell of the shed and the sounds of the storm around us. And Hades, ravaging me with his gaze.

He steps forward and snags the front of my shirt. In a quick motion, he rips it open. Buttons pop and scatter. And as much as it turns me on, I find myself attempting to tug it closed on instinct. His hands slide up my wrists.

"What did I tell you about hiding?"

"I'm dirty," I protest.

"Oh, I'm counting on it," he murmurs against my skin. "I expect you to be very, fucking, dirty."

He leaves my hands gripping the table on either side of my thighs, and he moves between them, kneading them hard as he kisses up my neck. His mouth feels like such a welcome relief. A small sigh escapes me as I shift into his touch. The rain is still coming off the roof in sheets, but we're barely undercover. My makeup feels ruined, my hair damp.

"We can't do this here."

"Says who?" he argues.

A scandalized laugh escapes me.

"Hades. I practically work here."

This time when his eyes flash, it's not with a challenge but a promise. He hooks his hands behind my knees and tugs me closer to him in a single, rough movement that makes my heart jump. Heat pools between my legs, sudden and aching. He massages the spot over the top of my jeans.

"Does it look like I give a fuck?" He unclasps the button of my pants and hooks his fingers into the waistband, dragging them down my hips, quick and hard. "You're mine."

With the added space he's created, he dips his hand inside my panties. I meet his mouth with a moan, move my hips to meet his touch.

"You're not going to fuck me here," I protest.

"Who said I'm going to fuck you?" he says, palming my breast over the top of my bra.

"Aren't you?" I breathe.

"No."

Fuck, I think.

I instinctively press into all the places he's touching me. Between my legs. At the spot where he's tracing the edge of my bra and then hooking a finger inside of it to seek out my nipple. Sensation thrums through me as he flicks it, smiling one of his most wicked smiles as it hardens into a tight, sensitive bud.

I sigh against his mouth. "I swear to the gods if you edge me right now, I will find the nearest spade and stab you with it."

He howls out a laugh. Then, he presses two fingers deep inside me, hooking them against my sweet spot and using them to tug me closer to the edge of the counter. With his free hand, he reaches for the wall behind me, grabbing a clean spade from the hook.

"Like this?" he says, waving it between us.

"Asshole," I chortle, clutching his shirt and dragging his mouth back to mine.

"Mmm, not the hole I was hoping for, but we can always pivot if you want."

My laugh melts into a whimper as he strokes me, hard and slow, before withdrawing his touch. He meets my protest with a kiss, and in one more tug, my pants slide off and land on the dusty floors beneath our feet. He turns the spade so that he's holding the very base of the handle above the shiny blade, then presses my chest so that my upper back meets the wall with enough force to make the tools clatter.

My lids are heavy as my eyes slide up to his.

"What are you doing?" I breathe.

He rubs the rounded end of the green plastic handle up and down between my legs, pressing the fabric of my underwear against me in a tantalizing way.

"Helping you out," he says, as he uses the handle to push my panties to the side. "I figured you'd want this… close. In case you decide you still want to stab me."

I gasp as the smooth plastic makes contact with the slickness between my legs. My head tips back as he presses it inside me.

"Oh my god, it feels so…"

Dirty. I feel so fucking dirty letting him do this, even though I know that the tools are in fact cleaned to almost surgical standards every evening before being put away.

"What if someone sees us?" I breathe.

"Then you'll have an awful lot of explaining to do about why you let me fuck you with a garden tool. Slash possible murder weapon."

I sigh with each of his movements, following the handle in and out, rolling my hips to meet his thrusts.

"Don't edge me and it won't be a problem."

The glimmer of his smile is villainous. He glances over his shoulder and reaches for one of the clusters of drying herbs that are attached to a line running through the center of the shed, held in place by a series of wooden planting clips. The opening in them is big enough that they won't crush the stems but tight enough that it can keep the small bundles secure. When he pinches the ends of the nearest wooden clip together, a drying bunch of basil falls to the ground.

"Hey," I protest. "You can't—"

I have barely reached forward when he presses his hand into my chest and pushes me back.

"I can," he says. "And you want me to."

He drags the clip between my breasts, and my heart speeds up when I realize what he's about to do. As I watch him, everything seems to happen in slow motion.

The way he snugs the clip under the straps of my bra, dragging them over my shoulders.

How he nudges the cups down until my nipples are peeking over the tops.

The heightened sensation as he rubs the wooden end over the hard, sensitive peaks.

"Or did you want me to stop telling you what you want?" he adds.

I moan as he snugs the opening of the clip until it fits perfectly around the bud of my nipple. It's not quite as snug as the metal clamps he used on our first night together, but when he tugs on it, the jolt of pleasure that surges through me is the same. Heat rises in my face as I curse.

"Yeah? You want me to stop acting like I know what you want?" he growls. "What you need?"

The thunder crashes, and the very air feels electric, and I moan again as he drives the handle of the spade deeper inside me.

"No," I manage. "I don't want you to stop."

When I throw my head back, it rattles the entire wall behind me. I writhe my hips against his touch. He pinches the next clip to my other breast, and I'm so grateful for the sounds of the storm to cover my moans as he flicks them. Left, right, right, left. He knows I go crazy when he plays with me like this, and he draws it out.

It makes no sense when his tongue finds my clit. I'm half-convinced I'll open my eyes and look down to see the spade jabbing uncomfortably into his neck in his current position, but he's angled it so the convex side is safely against his chest and the top of the handle is massaging my innermost need. And he licks me—not in that wandering way he sometimes does, but in the way that he knows will drive me home. I spread my legs wider for him, pressing my hips up to meet his mouth and digging a hand into his hair.

"I refuse... to ask... your permission for this," I pant.

"Your body is asking for it anyway." He flicks the garden clips. "Your hard nipples." He rocks the handle against the deepest point of my desire until I have to stifle a scream. "Your wet pussy." His tongue teases me again. "Come on, princess. You think I don't know you want me to make you come like a greedy whore? Take it. Take whatever the fuck you need."

"What I need," I say, grinding my hips up to meet his mouth, "is for you to shut the fuck up."

I don't know what I expect when I admit this, but it's not the absolute relief I feel when he buries his face against me with a groan, flicking his tongue against my clit and teasing his thumb against the exposed tips of my nipples. Every point of pleasure melts into the next, until I'm—

"Hades. I... *Fuck*."

The climax rushes through me, hot and hard and sweet. I come with my moans filling the small shed, my fingers gripping his damp hair, and the sounds of the rain falling off the tin roof reduced to a steady trickle.

He tosses the spade to the nearest workbench with a satisfied clatter before retrieving my pants from the floor. I'm still riding out the final surges of pleasure as he roughly threads my legs into the openings and tugs the jeans back up around my hips. It's a quick, purposeful motion that lifts me off my seat and sends the fabric taut against my sex. When he gives the waistband a few extra teasing yanks for good measure, I almost think I'm going to start coming again. He meets my whimper with a caress of his lips, kissing me as he works the zipper closed and refastens the button.

"What about you?" I murmur, still feeling warm and melty as he removes the clips from my sore nipples and slides the straps of my bra back onto my shoulders. "You didn't finish."

"Are you *still* arguing with me?"

A small, stubborn smile plays across my lips as I scrunch one side of my face.

"Maybe?"

"You are infuriating," he says, kissing the tip of my nose. "And I have every intention of fucking you. But we should probably get out of here before the weather clears."

We do our best to make ourselves presentable. He gathers my ruined shirt, and I slide my arms into the holes before tying the loose ends into a knot above my navel. While he adjusts himself in his pants, I sweep my damp hair from beneath my shirt collar. Thankfully there's no one in sight as we link hands and slosh our way through the muddy garden, leaving dirty footprints down the wet, winding path of the village.

"Do you want me to go?" I finally ask, my voice small.

"No. Of course not."

"Then why did you say it? You're not stupid. You had to know it would hurt me."

"Because I want you to think this through."

Annoyance flares in me again. "The fact that you think I haven't means you're still not listening."

He stops abruptly, tugging my hand so that I spin against his chest.

"Oh, I'm listening." When he sucks the spot beneath my ear, I gasp out a tiny sigh. "I listen to these incredibly, sexy sounds you make. I listen to your body, so I know exactly what you want. And I hear you when you say that today was shit, and nothing is fair, and you think I'm the same as all those other people who are using you."

I grab his face on either side so I can look him in the eyes, furrowing my brow. "I don't think you're the same. You're not using me. But you don't get to make choices for me."

"I don't think *you* were listening." He kisses the inside of my palm, trailing down my wrist. "Because I wasn't trying to make choices for you. I was asking you to consider all of your choices, because being here has to be your choice. An informed one."

I breathe out low and long, closing my eyes at the smooth way he caresses me. "Now you're calling me un-informed."

"You're still in the mood to argue?" he teases.

"No," I admit. "I dunno."

He levels his gaze with me. "Tell me what you want."

My mind is a tangled mess, so I shrug.

"Atrium?"

He raises an eyebrow. "That's what you want?"

I wrap both hands around his, sandwiching his one between my two.

"I want to give you what you want," I admit, a blush creeping up my neck.

"You never have to tell me what you think I want to hear. I hope you know that, Persephone. The truth. That's the only thing I ever ask."

"Okay," I say. "The truth is I'm... spent. And I just want to be alone with you. In your bed."

He smiles, kissing the top of my head. "In *our* bed."

"Okay, seriously? It's *you* who is arguing with *me*." My heart swells, and I shove him playfully. We fall into step again, sending a pair of small birds flying away from a nearby puddle. "But that's okay? If it's just us?"

It's not that we don't spend plenty of time alone, but in this moment, it's exactly what I need. The way that he knows me so innately wraps around my heart and tugs. I bite into my smile, tucking myself against him.

"More than okay," he says. "Especially since I plan to spread you open and make you come until you forget about this no good, terrible day."

Now, I don't argue. On this we absolutely agree.

14

I try to ignore the news, but by mid-winter, my mother's war is wearing on me.

First, it comes from the concerned emails sent by my skeleton crew off-season staff at Bounty. The cold hardy leafy greens are wilting, and the winter harvest of potatoes is coming in blighted. When it's the first location, I write it off as poor planning or bad luck. When the rest of them report the same situation, uneasiness spreads.

Then it hits the greenhouse vegetables. I receive pictures of tomatoes, peppers, and squash, rotting on the vine, as if the plants have no roots. When they pull them up, I receive the next chilling set of images. The stalks have come out of the ground so easily because they *don't* have roots. It's as if they've dissolved.

How can a plant grow to maturity without roots? And how does an otherwise healthy plant lose them?

"I don't know what it is," I tell Hades as we lie in the dark, watching the curtains make lazy shadows on the ceiling. "But whatever it is, it's bad."

"Have you talked with the gardeners here? They might have some insight."

"Yes. Essie. Tilda. Christoph. All of them. They've never seen anything like it either. They're just..."

Diseased.

This is the word that begins popping up on the news, followed quickly by *famine.* When I dare to check it, images of grocery store shelves, half-empty, fill up the feed. People swarm like locusts, buying up whatever they can, more than they could possibly need, in panic. It angers me as much as it chills me. Everyone has to eat.

I spend hours inspecting the village's greenhouses, terraced plots, and orchards, terrified of finding evidence that it's spread here, but our crops are healthy and the yield is as steady as ever. This should reassure me, but somehow it doesn't.

"You're going to make yourself sick, if you keep looking at this," Hades tells me gently, plucking the phone from my hands as he joins me for breakfast.

"I just..." The heavy feeling in my stomach grows, and it gives me the sensation of sinking, as if it's pulling me down to the very bottom of the river. My chest burns like I've been underwater too long, and I draw in a tight breath. "I think it's *her*."

His eyes search mine.

"Have you heard from her?"

"No, but this is a message, isn't it? It has to be."

As the pomegranate cuttings I propagated months ago and placed in large, decorative planters around the balcony of our bedroom begin to thrive, my hope slowly begins to wither.

When HMZ finally reports, Hades is outraged.

"*'Inside sources reveal this may be an act of agricultural warfare from across the Styx*'?!" he growls. "I swear I would gut Hermes myself if I didn't think he would turn it into news. Sniveling little bastard."

He launches the tablet against the wall. When it lands on the floor, I can see the spiderweb cracks across the screen. He drags a hand roughly across his face, as if the moment he sees it, he's disappointed in himself.

"I'm sorry," he says.

I've never seen him so angry, but after months of his benign response to my anxiety, I feel justified.

"It's okay," I reply, defeated. "I get it."

He sighs himself into the space beside me on the sofa, and I tuck my legs beneath me as I pull up Olympic News on my phone, only to find an anchor on the screen with my mother's photo in the bottom corner.

"*... amid growing concern from people like Demeter Bauer, Owner and CEO of Big Farma, who believes this is an act of war.*"

The image shifts to a recording of what looks to be an earlier press conference, held in one of the Big Farma board rooms where I used to play hide and seek as a child. My mother is standing behind the podium with the company's emblem on the front of it, three stalks of golden wheat. The podium itself is surrounded by vases of fresh poppies, so dark they look like blood. My mother's voice is her polished brand of calm-but-urgent as she speaks into the microphones surrounding her.

"*We have reasons to believe that Hades is responsible for this. It's an act of clear retaliation, because I have dared to shed a light on all the girls like my daughter Persephone, who have been taken hostage across the river.*

"*This villain is trying to shut me up by hitting us where it hurts, and he will not stop until every field lays dead and barren. He is a criminal, and he must pay for his crimes. Join me in my call to put an end to this famine and demand that my daughter be returned home safely and our livelihoods be restored.*"

A stifled sob works its way up my throat, and I gape at the screen.

"She can't do this," I stammer. "She can't! We'll tell them. We have to tell them all of this is bullshit!"

Hades shakes his head. "We don't play these games like they do across the river."

"Why not?" I demand. "Don't you want people to know the truth?"

"Death doesn't offer explanations, Persephone. It just *is*. People will speculate and make up stories about what goes on in the Underworld as they have since the beginning of time. If we start offering up certainties now, there are a lot more questions people will demand be answered. 'Why this person? Why me? Why now? What next?' We don't explain, and we don't negotiate."

It makes sense, and yet I don't want it to. I wrap my hand around his forearm like a lifeline, and he draws me against his chest. My tears come hot and fast, and I can't catch my breath.

"Why are they doing this?" I cry. "What could she possibly be gaining from this?"

"I don't know, princess."

"People are going to *die*."

"I know."

A hiccupping sob overtakes me, and I can barely force out the next words around the ache that sears through my chest. "They'll say it's what we wanted. What you wanted. More people. Across the river."

More people dead.

"I know." He rocks me in his arms, pressing his mouth to the top of my head. "I know."

He holds me as the waves of grief trash me until I'm spent on the shore. I hear his heartbeat steady under my ear as I cling to him, safe and kept, like an unbroken promise. All I want is to be with him. But there is a conflicting pull in my body, and it hurts like someone is attempting to remove my vital organs, because I know that there are other things I want as well.

I want to know that there's a healthy food supply across the river.

I want people to be able to feed their families.

I don't want anyone to die, least of all because of *me*.

My voice is hoarse and raw. "Why is life so hard?"

"You're asking the King of the Dead about life?" I can tell he's trying to tease, but his tone is heavy and his words are a dark rumble in his chest. "I don't know, sweet nymph."

Something akin to worry or anger or defeat furrows his brow. Perhaps some strange mix of all three. In the wake of the news, I feel myself going numb to the pain. My breath comes shallow and quiet, and I trace the lines of his bare chest, stroke the soft, dark hair, follow the curve of his muscled arm where it hooks around me.

"I think…" Tears well in my swollen eyes, choking me. "I think I have to…"

Go back.

The unspoken words hang between us, filling up the large room until I'm sure the weight of them will suffocate me. Hades snugs his finger beneath my chin and gently lifts my tear-streaked face to his. There's genuine pain in his eyes, like the ocean around a shipwreck, dark and somber. His lips find mine so gently.

"I know."

I spend three days trying to talk myself out of it. Three days drinking too much wine to numb the gut-wrenching pain. Three days attempting to enjoy all of the beautiful, sensual pleasures the palace has to offer. I stay in bed with Hades and rarely get dressed, fucking him until my whole body aches.

But every time a plate of food is set in front of me, and every time I walk through the rows of our healthy gardens, the weight pulls me down again, because I know I have no choice. By the time I'm standing at the edge of the river, misty with the sunrise that hasn't yet burned off the fog, I feel like my mind is caught in a body that is moving on auto-pilot.

Hades stands tall in his black clothes, looking as impeccable as ever, except that there are dark circles under his eyes, and his hair is a mess from the way he's been tearing at it the whole walk here. He smooths the lapels of the coat he helped me into before we headed for the river, tugging the dark wool tight. When his gaze meets mine, I'm convinced I might break.

"Please." My voice is a raspy whisper. "Tell me not to go."

"You know I can't do that." He draws my hand to his mouth and kisses it. "We don't take hostages here."

"I hate you for this," I murmur, but there's no venom in my tone, and his sympathetic eyes tell me he knows I don't mean it. "I'm going to miss you every second of every day."

"I'll miss you, too, little nymph. You have no idea."

I press my hands into his chest, reveling in the feel of him holding them tight against his warmth, against his heart. I know people across the river will swear he doesn't have one. How could the King of the Dead care more about life than the woman they've placed in charge of every crop within the known world?

"I'll come back. I'm going to fix this and be back. It'll only be a few weeks. A month tops."

When he holds my gaze, I can tell we both wonder if what I'm saying can even be done. This vow already feels desperate and broken.

"You have to go," he says. "The longer you stand here the closer I am to breaking all the rules and tying you up and never letting you leave—the whole world be damned. Please, Persephone. Go."

I'm not sure this controlled king has ever begged me for anything, and my knees almost collapse beneath me. The cracking in his voice splinters my heart. When I suck in my next shaky breath, all I can feel is the gaping hole in my chest.

I wipe my tears roughly and kiss him, trying not to think if it will be the last time, because I can't breathe when I consider it. When we pull apart, his lips brush my forehead with finality. Charon is waiting, but—always a stickler for keeping things on schedule—we both know he won't for much longer.

With unsteady feet, I cross back onto the ferry for the first time in months, where Juno is waiting for me. She wraps an arm around my shoulders like the kind of mother mine has never been—consoling and concerned—and it's perhaps the only thing holding me up. The wind over the water whips my hair across my face, and I don't bother to stop it, because it smells sweet like the waters of the Roman spa, where Hades took me on our final night together when I couldn't sleep, so he could make love to me under the stars.

By the time I gather my wild, windswept locks at the nape of my neck and look back across the shore, I can't see anything but hazy mist. Ahead of me, the buildings of the city stretch up in the cold-clear skies of almost-spring.

I shrug my shoulders up around my ears against the chill and dip my trembling hands into the warm pockets of my coat, fingering the embossed gold coin with the emblem of Hades—of my kingdom. In the other, I smooth my fingers over the small paper packets of seeds.

15

After spending nearly half a year in Hades's palace, my mother's mountaintop mansion reminds me of a tacky dollhouse. Juno pulls to a stop in front of the gates. The engine of her sleek, classy car idles as she peers up at it.

"You sure you don't want me to go with you?" she asks. "I feel like I'm feeding you to the wolves."

I shake my head. "My mother doesn't allow cameras here. The only surveillance is around the perimeter. She won't make a scene without an audience."

Juno leans across the seats and hugs my neck. Leaning into her is like pressing my face into an armful of clean laundry, all vanilla and lavender. She smells like home, somehow.

"If you need anything..." she tells me.

I swallow the knot in my throat, blinking past the burning feeling in my eyes like I've sucked saltwater up my nose.

"Take care of him?"

We both know, without the use of a name, which *him* I'm referring to. For the first time all morning, Juno's eyes go glossy with the threat of tears, and she nods.

"Of course. But please... take care of *yourself*."

When I step out into the cold, I can hear the engine of her car humming behind me while I press the button on the intercom and wait. The video screen comes to life, and I see the face of an unimpressed security guard.

"Yeah?" he says, barely looking at the camera.

"I'm here to see my mother."

At my words, the guard's image shifts closer. His eyes focus on me before growing wide. He fumbles the paper cup of coffee in his hands and spills some down his shirt. I wonder if it's hot, because he immediately curses.

"Holy—" he stammers.

The clamoring commotion in his small security office crackles through the speaker, and the shadows of the other guards slide across the screen as they rush to help him.

"Persephone Bauer," he stammers. "I've got... She's... She's here."

Suddenly, three people are gawking at me, arguing over each other. Finally, one of them hits a button on the control panel, and the gate begins to silently slide open. The heels of my boots click along the concrete as I trek up the driveway.

It's a funny feeling, being back from the dead. Doors open for me before I can reach them. Staff buzzes around, offering me beverages I don't accept and attempting to take my coat for me, which I also refuse. I feel like royalty—right up until the moment that I sit down in the stiff, leather armchair across the wide desk in my mother's home office. It swallows me so that my feet barely touch the ground, which makes me feel like a little girl.

"I'm glad to see you've come to your senses," she finally says.

Though I'm sure she'll sell it to the press later, this is not a tearful reunion. She purses her lips and steeples her fingers at her chin, looking me over like nothing about my appearance pleases her.

"I've scheduled a press conference at noon, but we'll need to push it to three. I didn't realize you were going to show up with your hair looking like you've rolled out of some filthy sex dungeon—"

"No," I interrupt.

She quirks her head as if she doesn't understand the meaning of this word.

"No?"

"You got what you wanted. I came back. But I'm not doing a press conference."

She laughs. "I don't think you're in the position to make demands. You put our family's reputation—our entire livelihood—in jeopardy."

"And you put *everyone's* livelihood in jeopardy. If you put me on camera, I will tell every soul that you're responsible for this so-called 'famine.'"

Her eyes shift to dark, smoldering embers that look ready to sear through me.

"You can't hide out at home. They'll want to see proof you're back."

"Tell them... I'm too traumatized for public appearances." I wave a hand, as if it doesn't matter. "Tell them whatever you want. Make things up. Isn't that what you're best at?"

"I'll give you a month," she says. "To rest and recover. But we're scheduling a big banquet for spring, to announce our treatment for the blight. We've already begun applying it with great success. We're trying to get through some of that ridiculous regulatory red tape, but it's as good as done."

I roll my eyes, scoffing out a bitter laugh. "I'm sure. It's easy to solve a problem you created, isn't it?"

"I want you there."

We stare at each other over the desk, like a middle school contest. Anger flares within me, and it's the first thing I've felt all day that isn't agony. I hold onto it, almost scared that if it disappears I won't be able to feel anything at all.

I finger the packet of seeds in my pocket again. A month is enough time to distribute and plant them. Enough time to sow distrust and dissent. Hopefully enough time to convince people of the actual truth.

"Fine. Consider it done."

My apartment feels exactly as I left it. The cleaning staff kept coming even after I disappeared—paid every week via an automatic transfer that I couldn't bear to cut off, knowing how hard times have gotten for everyone around here— but it all feels wrong. The brightly colored clothes hanging neatly in the closet don't resemble anything I want to wear. The bed feels at once too small and too empty. And when I lie down on it and stretch my arms out on either side of me, there's no solid, warm body there to meet my touch.

I curl myself around my pillow and cry until the muscles of my face ache. When the tears finally run dry, my eyes are so swollen I can barely see, but I still find myself sobbing, because I don't know how to do this. Any of this. Win a war against my mother. Carry on without him.

How do I live without the King of the Dead?

I wish I could call him, but I know that I brought all the traditional lines of communication back across the river with me. The few messages he sends are carried by the murder of crows that frequents his balcony at the palace. I can't say he trained them to do his bidding as much as be-friended them. Regardless, none of them make their way to my window. The absence of them feels like intentional silence, and I wonder if the season I spent across the Styx was just a dream, much like the ones that haunt me as I spend days in bed. I slip in and out of them with each one more fevered than the last.

When I finally decide I can't languish inside anymore, I learn that the sidewalk in front of my building is crowded with reporters, waiting for a glimpse of me. I feel more like a prisoner in this apartment than I ever did across the river. I end up walking the hallways and stairs to give myself something to do—some sense of forward motion.

That's how I find the unmarked door to the roof.

It's late afternoon. The sky is orange and the whole city smells slightly humid, as if you could breathe deep enough and catch hints of spring. If I squint, I swear I can see all the way to the river from here. I try to get a better view, but when my hips meet the block ledge that's intended to keep people like me from falling off, I still can't see the dark, winding water.

I look down at the street and sidewalk below. I wonder how far down it is. The concrete blocks are rough beneath my hands. I bite my bottom lip and lean further over, counting the windows to determine how many stories up I am. The next thought creeps up the back of my neck like a whisper.

I could do it. Step right over the edge.

The idea makes me feel tingly and panicked, but there's a dark part of me that registers it's my fastest way back to him. Could he save my soul from the Underworld? Would he be able to bring me back to life if I did something so rash and stupid? Or would he show up before my feet ever left the ledge and save me, the way he did that morning in the street?

"What are you doing?" a woman's voice says.

I jolt with a start, and for a heart-flailing moment, I'm terrified that I could fall over. I stumble away from the edge, desperate to put distance between me and the possibility. When I turn, I expect a security guard, but I'm met with a petite woman in scrubs. I get the sense that she doesn't recognize me, but I adjust the bill of the baseball cap I've taken to wearing every time I leave the safety of my apartment.

I clear my throat. "I was looking for the, um, cameras. To see if I could see them from here."

She's wearing a zip-up sweatshirt over her light blue scrubs, and she looks like maybe she just got off shift somewhere. Her shoes are those squishy rubber ones. Her dark hair is pulled into a short, spriggy ponytail. And she's holding a bottle of strawberry beer. She shrugs it, like it's the question mark at the end of her next statement.

"Can you?"

"No."

"Good." She takes a satisfied swig, noticing the way my eyes track the movement. "Want a drink? I've started coming up here for happy hour because it's too much of a hassle to leave."

"Um, yeah. Sure," I nod.

When I fall into step beside her, she adds, "You know HMZ is down there? They're actually sleeping on the sidewalk. I think one of them has a camp stove. Shit is crazy."

I sigh through my nose.

"Crazy is an understatement."

"I'm Hesperides," she offers. "But friends call me Espe."

"I'm..."

She quirks one corner of her mouth.

"I know who you are."

"Right." The tentative hope in me sinks. So much for anonymity. "You just got off work?"

"Yeah. I'm a family practitioner. Over at Hera Clinic."

"Oh," I say, feeling the bright glimmer of recognition. "That's awesome. I know Juno."

Espe's brows draw together as she gives me an incredulous smile.

"You know Juno Childs," she deadpans.

I had no idea until this moment that her last name was Childs, but I gesture in the affirmative.

"Yeah."

Espe smushes her mouth into an upside down smile, nodding in a subtly impressed way.

"Is she as awesome as they say? In person, I mean."

"She's pretty great. You've never met her?"

"No. Not really. Well, I mean, once, sort of. She was my idol, growing up. You know she actually saved my sister from this crazy hemorrhage, after she had her second kid. None of the other doctors caught it, but Juno was on site that day and... When she walked into the waiting room, she was covered in blood – my sister's blood, I guess – and I was so sure she was about to tell us that we lost her. Anyway. *That* day. That's the reason I became a doctor. Man, I wanted to be just like her. Cheesy, right?"

"Not at all."

When we round the large block structure that surrounds the top of the stairwell, I can see a small collection of mismatched folding chairs set up around a wooden crate, which seems to be functioning as a coffee table. Espe sinks into one and opens the small cooler, passing me an ice cold bottle.

"Thanks," I murmur.

Tucked away from the view of the rooftop door, this little seating area is adjacent to rows of empty wooden boxes. I furrow my brow. They almost look like...

"Are those planters?"

"Oh. Yeah. With this crisis and everything, a few of us in the building tried to see if we could get anything to grow. We read online you can plant potatoes and they would turn into more potatoes, or something? Anyway, it didn't work."

It would have worked, I think. *But not if you're using Big Farma's potatoes.* They genetically modified them to only grow with the addition of certain chemical compounds, to prevent 'theft.'

As my eyes scan the available boxes, my brain begins to take inventory of everything that's here, everything I have, and everything we'll need. The thought takes root: if I can't leave the building to grow my contraband produce, maybe I could grow it here.

I drag my gaze back to Espe.

"Do you want help? Trying again, I mean?"

I try to keep my tone light. After all, I don't know this girl. Just because she idolizes Juno and offered me a beer doesn't make us friends, or even allies, but for the first time in too long, a foreign feeling dances through my chest.

Hope.

It swells when she shrugs.

"Sure. I don't have much else to do. It's kind of a pain in the ass to leave the building with your camera crew lurking around."

I sigh out a laugh. "Tell me about it."

She tips the beer to her mouth, scanning the empty boxes.

"So, you can tell me to fuck off if you want, but all that stuff they're saying. About across the river. And the 'agricultural war.' And you being..." She inclines her head, letting me fill in that particular blank. "Is it true?"

The latent ache in my chest twists. I suck my bottom lip between my teeth, scared if I open my mouth that I'll tell her *everything*. Like I won't be able to stop the story from pouring out of me. My eyes well, and the force of holding back the emotion becomes as stinging as the feeling of holding back the words.

Eventually, I shake my head.

"Yeah. I didn't think so."

When I meet her gaze, she offers me a resigned nod. There's a solidarity there, as if I've just confirmed something she's always known but that no one will let her admit is true. As if the truth is only something that can be owned by powerful people, not by two twenty-somethings sitting on a barren rooftop.

"So," she says, propping her feet on the makeshift coffee table and scanning the scene. "Where do we start?"

16

It's ironic that the underground movement I start, sown with seeds from the Underworld, is actually taking root on rooftops. Espe's gardening club is a hodgepodge of other building residents, which I'm introduced to over the next week. Some are in their twenties and thirties—like the young couple from the second floor, the tech guru from the fourth, and the barista/DJ/spoken word poet from the fifth—but a few are older, like birdwatching besties Barb and Bianca, who've spent a lot of time hanging out on the roof since retirement. Despite their differences, they all show up with beverages or snacks or music in tow, and they are always excited about the day's tasks.

Planting. Weeding. Hauling fresh soil up the stairs. Even the days that leave them sweaty and dirt-smudged find them smiling. It's not the most conventional dynamic, but it works.

Espe in particular is insatiable. It's not really gardening she's craving, but *change*. Or maybe, the power to change things. As soon as we get the apartment garden going, she's already asked me to check with Juno to see if we can use the roof space at Hera Clinics.

"Do you know what you're doing?" Juno asks when I call. I hear her smile on the other end of the phone.

It hangs between us. I know what she means. Do I realize I'm advancing my position as an enemy in this war with my mother? I didn't start it, but it seems I'm committed to fighting it, for better or worse.

"Not really," I admit.

"Well, at least you're honest," she laughs. "Tell Espe yes, they can use the roof space. The main hospital is the largest, but if they want, they can use the smaller clinics, too. If anyone asks, I'll blame the board and their 'commitment to sustainability clause' or whatever."

I smile, but it's sad around the edges, because talking with Juno always makes me think of being across the river, which subsequently makes me think of *him*. The same way I'm thinking of him now, as I stand at the edge of the roof.

A shock of cold touches the back of my arm, and I spin around.

Espe laughs apologetically at my surprise. "You okay?"

"Yeah," I lie.

She offers me the unopened beer in her hand, fresh from the cooler.

"You hanging out tonight? We were thinking of getting a card game going. Dani is still desperate to beat Barb, and even though I think we all know how that's going to go, it might be fun."

"Sounds it," I smirk. "Unfortunately, I have a thing."

"A thing?"

"A family thing." It's the vaguest explanation for Big Farma's spring banquet, which is being hosted in one of the city's swankiest hotel ballrooms, but it makes the way I scrunch my nose in abject disgust make more sense. "Maybe next time?"

"Of course," she nods. "Standing invitation."

I head downstairs with the sun setting and go through the motions of getting dressed in the long, tulle gown my mother sent over. It's bright green, like the shoots of the contraband plants that have sprouted over the past few weeks. The bodice and skirt are adorned with tiny, spring flowers. It occurs to me when I meet my own reflection, with my cheeks bright with blush and my large brown eyes as wide as a doe's, that I look like a princess.

Patience, princess.

Chills run through me. If I close my eyes, he's almost here. I can almost feel his breath on the back of my neck, hear the deep timbre of his teasing words. A lump forms in my throat, and my next few breaths are tight with longing, because I miss him, right down to my bones.

I've gotten into the habit of constantly watching for crows, but even when I spot one, I can't tell if it's a message from him or just a curious bird, hoping to feed or entertain himself in an urban landscape. If their swirling flight paths and off-key calls are supposed to communicate something, I can't decipher what it is.

I wish I could talk to him.

I smooth my thumb over the coin that he pressed into my palm that last morning, when my skin was still warm with his scent and my body was still thrumming with the contentment of being tangled up with him. A few weeks ago, I managed to add a tiny hole and thread it with a long, delicate chain.

When I slip it over my head, I'm grateful to find it fits perfectly beneath the modest V neckline of the dress my mother selected. The medallion is warm against my skin, nestled between my breasts, grazing the bottom of my sternum. It's perhaps the only thing that gives me the confidence to walk downstairs, fight through the cluster of reporters, and duck into the hired car that takes me across town.

Throughout the drive, I wonder what they'll write about me, and my mother, and the fact that Big Farma is hosting this lavish event despite the fact that the food supply has still been unstable at best, while farmers battle the blight that is still being attributed to Hades, and grocery shelves sit half-empty, and the talk of ration cards spreads.

I'm sure the food at this event will be decadent. My mother isn't one to spare expense, as evidenced by the red carpet vibe at the hotel entrance. The wide terraced stairs leading to the main doors are littered with photographers, snapping flashbulb shots of people in sweeping gowns and sharp suits. Columns of light reach up into the inky night sky, drawing us in like moths to a flame.

I hear my name from every angle as I step out of the car.

"Persephone!"

"How does it feel being home?"

"Who are you wearing this evening?"

"What's your plan for seeing Bounty through the blight?"

"How do you feel knowing that your captor has not been brought to justice?"

I dodge them as best I can with a bowed head and a demure smile, but I can hear Hades's voice in my ear.

No hiding.

I lift my chin, taking sure steps. The sounds of their questions disappear. I climb the stairs and drift towards the elevators, where bellmen check names off of exclusive lists and escort us to the top floor ballroom that provides a 365° view of the city. The night sky stretches beyond the walls of windows. There's a dark hazy ribbon in the distance, and I convince myself it's the river.

My heart dips.

I seem to always be tracking it these days, as if the palace across it is my true north. I want to draw closer to the windows and imagine I can see the Roman spa with its cozy courtyard, lush bougainvillea, and Hades, naked and glistening.

A server steps in front of me, blocking my view and pulling my attention back into the bustling ballroom.

"Hors d'oeuvres, miss?"

My startled gaze drops to the platter, and I'm so shocked to see the crostini with bright strawberries and fresh basil on top that I stop and stare.

Everyone in this room—besides me, I suppose—is here to raise a rallying cry against the blight, and no one seems to question the fact that they're being served ripe, untouched fruit. The clinking of glassware and the din of conversation feels suddenly too loud. Anger surges through me.

"Miss?" the server prompts. "Are you all right?"

I perhaps mean to respond, but I feel the moment my mother spots me across the crowd like a prickle against the back of my neck. When my gaze flicks to hers, she beams. The guests part for her without being prompted, and I wonder if that's what power is: the world bowing to your wishes before you even have to ask.

"Ah, here she is! My beautiful, brave girl."

She welcomes me with the kind of open arms that can only be for show. When she pulls me into a hug, she smushes my face uncomfortably against the side of hers. I do my best to keep the polite smile I've been practicing plastered on, but it doesn't reach my eyes.

"Here I am," I offer.

She shines in her gold dress, as vibrant as the sunset across a wheat field.

"I was just telling Senator Libera how excited you are to meet him." She smiles as if I should know who this is, and he materializes as if on cue. "You two actually went to university together."

The man grinning at me looks easily fifteen years older than I am. His dark hair is faintly peppered. The corners of his eyes are marked with subtle crow's feet. There's an old money arrogance oozing off of him. I wonder if my mother means that we simply graduated from the same school or were there at the same time, because the latter feels unlikely.

"Small world," I say.

He accepts two glasses of champagne from a passing tray without acknowledging the server. The first he offers to me, and the second he tips to his thin smile. His eyes remain trained on me over the rim of the fluted glass.

"Your mother also tells me your business has been struggling since the blight set in," he remarks.

It's true. I haven't offered the smuggled seeds to my locations at Bounty. The reality is that I'm not sure who I can trust, and I don't want my mother to get wind of the fact that there are plants that aren't susceptible to whatever disease her scientists cooked up before they've had a chance to bear fruit. The only way my plan works is keeping her in the dark long enough to have solid, undeniable proof that her plants were intentionally poisoned, which means keeping my mouth shut. One wrong word and her goons will raid my gardens and the news media will write off anything I say as a wild conspiracy theory.

Everything as it stands right now is just that—a theory. But I don't just want to *tell* the truth, I want to *show* it. I need the kind of truth people can sink their teeth into. The kind that dribbles down your chin like a ripe tomato. That fills your mouth like a sweet burst of strawberry.

So as much as I want to stand in the middle of this crowd and shout, '*my business is actually* thriving *because I haven't sold my soul to the devil like the rest of you*', I hear myself saying, "Yes. It's been a challenging time."

"Challenging indeed." The senator nods, but there's a gleam in his eye. "But what are challenges, if not an opportunity for the bold to rise to the occasion?"

I meet his gaze, feeling unsettled but unwilling to be ruffled. He and my mother exchange a conspiratorial look.

"The bold, and the *best*," she says, raising her glass to him. "Those are the ones who make history. Wouldn't you agree, Persephone?"

I gesture with my glass, giving an even smile and secretly relishing the idea that their comeuppance is close.

"I tend not to concern myself with history. After all, some of us have to be focused on the future."

Their canned laughter grates across my nerves, and I take a slow, satisfied sip of bubbles when I see the spark of annoyance behind my mother's eyes.

Someone behind the elaborate podium at the head of the room announces that we should take our seats for dinner. I have a mental list of everything I have to do to make it through this evening, and I tick this one off.

Ignore the reporters and make it inside. Check.

Don't kill anyone during cocktail hour. Check.

After the plated dinner, a few boring speeches, and a round of dessert, I'll be back in the car and in the quiet of my own apartment. If I'm lucky, the raucous card game might still be raging on the roof. The thought that I am only a couple of hours from drinking a beer in an old sweatshirt, laughing with new friends, sitting among planters of hearty sprouts in the crisp night air fortifies me.

Then my mother smiles. It's one of those lethal upturns at the corners of her pursed mouth that promises I won't like whatever comes next. She places a beseeching hand on the arm of the man standing beside me.

"Senator, won't you join us at our table? Persephone's plus one couldn't make it, so there's an extra seat. You'd be doing us a favor, balancing out the group."

Of course, my invitation hadn't come with a plus-one. Somehow, I get the feeling this man expected that. The flower in his lapel matches my dress, and the moment I see it, I know this was a setup. The anger spreading through my chest threatens to rip me apart. My limbs vibrate with the desire to detonate and blow this place to bits, but a dreadful certainty anchors me to the spot.

I am trapped.

I am trapped because this was a trap. One that I walked right into. Willingly.

Stupidly.

The senator replies without missing a beat.

"It would be my pleasure." He offers me his arm. "Shall we?"

I swallow past the bile rising in my throat and steel my nerves, praying that he can't feel the way my hand is trembling through the sleeve of his jacket. The words feel like shards of glass in my mouth.

"It seems we shall."

17

What game is my mother playing? Which piece am I in this puzzle? I agonize over these lingering questions as we're served dinner, which is a show of excess that borders on grotesque.

Plump, golden game hens, brushed with herbs. Thick, fluffy mounds of potatoes that smell like warm butter. Bright yellow lemon slices. Roasted asparagus stalks that do not remotely resemble the flimsy, wilted bundle of stems I saw two people fighting over in a recent grocery store video that went viral.

I don't have the appetite for any of it: the extravagant meal, the senator at my side, my mother's many deceits. I shift in my seat and wonder how many families are going to bed hungry tonight as the guest speakers prattle on about disease, agricultural warfare, *death*.

During the brief interludes, the senator makes polite conversation. I do my best to keep the conversation off of me. It's a skill I learned early on, attending these events. People love to talk about themselves, and as long as I keep the questions flowing, they usually don't notice that I've offered nothing of myself. I learn that his given name is Christopher, though his friends call him Topher.

Of course they do, I think.

"Well. I suppose that makes me Phoney," I remark.

By the time wine glasses are being refilled and my mother is stepping behind the microphone, I've learned he has a family home in the countryside with a flourishing winery, despite this recent season's setbacks. He's also quick to boast that he owns the penthouse in this very hotel, which does nothing except further twist the knot in my stomach, because it feels like a come on – and a sleazy one, at that. I fantasize about stabbing him in the thigh with my salad fork.

Applause draws me back.

Everything about my mother glows when she takes the podium. Her signature gold dress glitters in the modest spotlights, but it's really her smile that dazzles. To be in the midst of an alleged war, she's surprisingly effusive, suspiciously sure. With the graceful lift of her hand, the applause recedes into the rapt quiet of people with their mouths full of exquisitely exclusive food and drink.

"Thank you, all," she beams. "Your generous contributions this evening will go a long way in helping us tackle the many agricultural challenges facing our country today. And with the support of some of our country's top lawmakers, I'm excited to announce that we are on track to gain special emergency provisions that will allow us to implement our treatment for this horrid disease in commercial fields as quickly as next week. We're lobbying for the government to subsidize this project in a joint effort of private and federal sectors to stabilize our farms and restore our food supply."

The response is momentous. People are abuzz—cheering, celebrating, congratulating each other on a war well-fought and won. It's amid this bubbly rush that I realize the man next to me doesn't look surprised. He takes another bite of his chicken, chewing smugly and washing it down with a swig of wine. Some strange mix of dread and satisfaction seeps into me when my mother wades back to our table and I catch him giving her that same crinkly-eyed look they exchanged earlier. I guarantee if I did enough sleuthing, I would discover his name at the top of the list of lawmakers supporting this change. I wonder how much he stands to benefit from this.

Another wave of anger churns in my stomach. I think I'm going to be sick.

I excuse myself, retreating to the open air rooftop I spotted earlier. The cool breath of evening is a welcome relief from the heat of too many bodies. I lean my forearms against the rail, tipping my head to the night sky.

I can pick it out easily from here: my stars, the ones Hades gave me that very first night in the Roman spa, seven pinpricks of light in a sea of ocean blue. The memory is tangled up with the taste of honeyed rum and the feel of Hades's arms around my waist.

"Some girls prefer diamonds," I'd teased.

"Diamonds only shine when they catch the light. Stars are light. They're also maps. They're stories."

"Mm. And what story do these stars tell about me?"

"A beautiful maiden who wandered into the arms of darkness," he purred.

I felt weightless in his strong arms, in the silky water. My fingers had traced the outline of his jaw. My lips had found his with gentle intensity.

"Where do they lead?"

"Mm, depends on the season. In the autumn and winter, they lead here. In the spring, they head back north."

"Why not pick some that are always here? Ones we can hold onto."

"You want to always be in one place?" he teased. "What's a story without a journey?"

"Mm. Tell me, Hades. What's your story?"

"Haven't you heard? I'm the villain. Always the villain."

I remember the way his heart beat under my palms. Remember the way he groaned when my lips met his. Remember the sound of my voice, dancing soft between us.

"You're not the villain in my story."

Behind me, a door opens, letting the sounds of the party drift outside.

"There you are," my mother says. "What are you doing out here? We need you back inside."

When I look up, she's already turning on her heel, so certain I'm going to follow. My voice cuts through the night, bringing her up short.

"When were you going to tell me?" I say.

"Tell you what?"

"That you faked a famine so you could get the government to loosen the regulations on your chemical compounds and pour taxpayer money into your company."

She glances around in irritation, but it's clear we're the only ones outside. Through the wall of windows, the choreography of dinner is still going strong. Guests talk animatedly, laughing and nodding. Servers buzz about, preparing to clear plates as they empty. A towering cart is being wheeled out of the kitchen, boasting an ornate array of desserts. Still, she lowers her voice, drawing so close I can smell the champagne on her breath.

"I don't have to tell you anything. I did what I had to do to pull us out of the mess you made," she growls. "Your little tryst across the Styx could have ruined us, but I've spun this into a story that everyone can rally behind. I've given them a common enemy. Promised them redemption."

"You're exploiting people," I scoff. "That man, *Topher*, seems to think he's getting a lot out of this."

She sneers. "You best see to it that he does."

Her words hit me like a slap. The blood rushes to my face, quick and hot.

"You can't *sell* me to him."

"You wanted a cure? You wanted people to have food to eat? These things come at a price."

"What would you have me do, Mother? Date him? *Marry* him?"

"Once we get our government funding and emergency approvals, I don't care what you do. Until then, you'd best make Topher believe that you're invested in his happiness, or people will starve, and your little garden project will be through."

Her gold skirts sweep behind her as she stalks for the door. The din of the evening grows louder as she swings it open and disappears again as it slow-closes behind her.

I'm left with the thudding of blood in my ears and the faint hum of traffic, somewhere down below. I close my eyes, hoping to quell the emotion rising within me like floodwater.

I came back for this. I left Hades for *this*. To fight this war. To make things better. And with every step I feel as though I'm two behind, struggling to make it across the finish line before my mother officially crushes my spirit and everything goes to shit. But the truth is, I can't make the gardens grow any faster. I have to let nature take its course.

Something nearby pings against the metal railing. In the dark, I almost can't see the crow's large, black body. He skips closer in a funny, sideways shuffle until he's directly in front of me. He quirks his head, peering at me with one of his black eyes.

I realize I'm frozen in the spot, blinking at him. It can't be one of Hades's familiars. There's nothing clipped to his feathers. No little scroll clutched in his talons. This isn't a message for me, but I swallow hard, wishing like hell it was.

"Tell him I'm figuring it out," I whisper. "Tell him I'll find my way back to him."

He tilts his head like he understands. Or perhaps he's wondering what strange human would imagine she could talk to a crow. With a flurrying flap of wings, the black bird sails away, disappearing in a diving swoop over the streetlight glow of the city.

By the time the dancing starts, I can easily escape without notice. I'm close, too, edging my way along the dancefloor and brushing palm fronds out of the way, when Topher catches my wrist.

"Going so soon?" he says. "I was hoping you'd do me the honor of a dance."

When he draws closer, I realize he smells like sickeningly expensive cologne and stale booze. I'm too close to the wall to back away, and I end up pinned between him and an oversized palm.

"If you've seen me dance, you'd know it wouldn't be much of an honor. I'm a terrible partner," I demur, eyeing the exit.

"I'm sure you'd make a fine partner." His voice crawls across my skin. "In fact, I'm sure you learned a thing or two across the river. I'd love to find out."

When his fingers graze my arm, I attempt to side step. His grip tightens around my bicep, holding me in place.

"Let me go," I say, my voice lethally low.

"Isn't this what you like? Being held hostage?" he challenges. "I heard you're a stunning sex slave."

Every nerve in my body screams that I have to get away from him, and I don't care if I have to burn down the building—or knee him in the balls—to do it. At this moment, a tall, broad man crowds us, smoothing his hand around my other arm.

"Persephone, darling," he says genially.

When I meet his bright green gaze, it takes everything in me not to collapse into his arms.

"Adonis," I say. "What are you—?"

"Sorry I'm late. I got stuck in traffic." He gives me a knowing wink.

Topher's voice is hard, but his possessive touch has mercifully disappeared. He extends his hand. "I don't think we've been introduced."

"I'm—"

"He's my date," I interject. "My plus one."

The senator gives a humorless chuckle.

"Sorry, sport. It seems I took your spot a few hours ago," he says smugly. "We were just about to share a dance."

"Since you've had all evening, I hope you don't mind if I cut in," Adonis says, flashing him one of those easy, beautiful smiles. "I've got to make up for the fact I missed dinner." To me he adds, "If you'll have me?"

My hand finds the crook of his arm with a grateful squeeze.

"Of course."

When he guides me away from Topher's heavy glare, I can barely feel my feet. We find ourselves in the center of the dancefloor, deep enough into the crowd of swaying couples that I can no longer feel the senator's outrage bearing down on me.

The feel of Adonis's strong arms looped chastely around my waist is a welcome relief, and I lean into it, following his lead until our footsteps match the music.

"What are you really doing here?" I ask.

He gives me a lopsided grin. "Didn't you know there's paparazzi outside? The cameras love a pretty face."

I laugh in spite of myself.

"How've you been, Your Highness?"

"Not great." I tuck myself against him so I can lower my voice. "Have you seen him?"

He brings his mouth close to my ear in a way that would appear to any onlooker that he's trying to whisper sweet-nothings over the sound of the music.

"I've been across the river, but no. No one has seen him much. People are saying he's lovesick."

I'm not sure which is worse: the thought of Hades in the atrium, entertaining girls the same way he entertained me that first night, or the idea of him spending all of his time completely alone.

"He's not the only one," I murmur.

Adonis meets my gaze.

"I take it you aren't dating that creep over there?"

"No. He's a sleazy set-up by my mother. Some sort of sick power play," I grimace. "If you hadn't shown up, I... Well, I might have had to grab the nearest steak knife and unalive him."

"Queen of the Dead. It suits you." Adonis's laugh vibrates against the hand I've laid across his chest. "Maybe we should get out of here before you're forced to commit homicide."

I can't deny that I'm desperate to escape this party, but it's never as simple as that.

"Where would we go?"

"Wherever two old friends go to catch up."

His tone is genuine, and everything about this feels like the easy comfort of friendship, of a shared knowledge, an understanding. As charming and handsome as Adonis can be, he isn't trying to lay any of it on me, and I may be the only woman in all of Olympus who would be relieved at this.

"You know if we leave here, the cameras are going to see us," I say. "People are going to think we're... together."

"Is that really such a bad thing right now?" he queries. "It might shut your mother up for a while. Deter that douchewad from talking to you again."

I smile in spite of myself. In my mind, I've already agreed. I can picture us escaping to the waiting car and speeding through city streets, laughing in the privacy of the backseat and leaving this night completely behind.

It's not my mother I worry about, really; my plans are already in motion to uproot everything she's done, so long as I can keep her in the dark for a little longer. But I wonder what Hades would think if he saw us together.

I don't know that Hades is following the news at all. He obviously doesn't take calls or emails or texts across the river. There's no way to get in touch with him—unless you count whispering wishes to random crows, pretending they could somehow reach him. But I can almost imagine someone tossing this tidbit his way, showing him still photos of the two of us, and I wonder if he would falsely believe that I'd moved on.

No, I think.

Whatever he and I had—whatever we *have*—runs so much deeper. It seems to exist somewhere beyond petty jealousy and assumptions. It's written in the stars. And an escape sounds like a balm to my soul.

It may be wishful thinking to imagine that this will stop my mom's plot with the senator in its tracks, but I meet Adonis's gaze with a wistful smile.

"There *is* a car waiting..." I venture.

He threads his fingers through mine and squeezes with encouragement. "And I've always said a photo op is a terrible thing to waste."

With a gentle tug, he guides me toward the exit.

18

The city streets slide past the darkly tinted windows of the hired car in a blur of buildings, signage, and lights. The sleek towers of downtown give way to the narrow storefronts of Old Town. This district was once known for its cozy restaurants and practical shops, and later for its abandoned storefronts when business shifted into newer neighborhoods. In the past few years people have returned, seeking out its affordable loft-style apartments, late-night music venues, and non-conformist clientele. This makes it an unlikely place for me to run into anyone I know—and a mercifully unlikely place for anyone to give a damn about filming me, even when I show up in evening wear.

Adonis gives directions to the driver, and we wind up at a bar with a speakeasy feel, where the exposed brick walls glow with colored lights and his handsome smile secures us a table in a VIP area.

"You weren't kidding about that face," I murmur.

"A blessing and a curse," Adonis muses. "So, tell me, Your Highness. Why are you here?"

The server appears and leaves us with crisp drink menus. The velvet rope he lets himself through is hardly needed this early in the evening. The sparse crowd and the band setting up make it seem like this place won't come alive for a few hours at least. After spending the evening in that crowded hotel ballroom, it's welcome all the same.

"You brought me here. Don't you remember?" I tease.

He gives me an even look. "You know what I mean."

I swell with a breath, because I know *exactly* what he means.

"It's... complicated."

Adonis's gaze dips pointedly to my chest.

For a brief moment, confusion muddles my consciousness. If I didn't know any better, I'd swear he's ogling me.

He leans forward, and my heart lurches—with shock, and annoyance, and something akin to the sudden urge to smack him for impropriety—then he slips a single finger along my collarbone and snags the delicate gold chain, drawing the necklace out of hiding. The warm coin with the stamped emblem dangles at the bottom. He lets it fall against my bodice, allowing the weight of its meaning to pass a shared understanding between us.

"I saw the way you two were together, and I was sure nothing on heaven or earth could pull you apart. So, forgive me, but you're going to have to do a little better than that."

I smooth my thumb over the emblem of Hades like a touchstone before tucking it back into my neckline. I roll the words around in my mouth, chewing the inside of my lip as if I could reshape them, or perhaps work the truth into something more palatable.

"People were going to die," I admit. "If I stayed."

His expression darkens.

"I heard something about that. So, it's true?"

"I'm not sure what you heard but... yeah, probably."

He accepts this with a serious nod. "How long then?"

"How long what?"

"Until you can go back."

He says it so matter-of-factly that I'm taken aback. Every moment that I'm not thinking about setting up new secret gardens—or actively working myself to exhaustion in the current network of secret gardens—I'm fantasizing about going back. But the longer I'm here, the more that's what it feels like: a faraway fantasy. I'm not as anonymous as I once was, and I can't ferry back and forth as I please, especially when I can't leave my apartment building without half of Olympus tracking my every move. Hell, I wouldn't be surprised if the hired driver had already alerted my mother—or HMZ—where he dropped us, and this is not half as exciting a place as the river Styx.

At this point in the game, I can't risk undoing everything I've already done. I haven't worked this hard plotting and planting to see my gardens get raided. I didn't sit through that terrible dinner and make small talk with Topher only to broadcast to my mother that I'm not actually playing by her rules. No, I need her to believe I'm under her thumb so that she doesn't expect what comes next. I need her to underestimate me. For now, that means keeping my feet on Olympus soil.

"I don't know," I say. The truth of it sits like a stone in my stomach, anchoring me down.

The server returns with a bottle of wine. He corks it in such a positively seductive way, cutting Adonis sidelong glances, that I'm sure he's hoping to steal him away from me. Given the smirk on Adonis's face, I'd suspect he's hoping the same. He watches the server go before clicking the edge of his glass to mine and taking a pensive draw.

"How can I help?"

I blink. "You want to help?"

His smirk splits into a broad laugh.

"What else? Don't insult me by acting like I rescued you from that creepy old man just to whisk you across town and hit on you."

"I'm not acting like that!" I defend. My smile simmers, and I finger the stem of my glass with a wistful expression. "I dunno. I feel like I'm drowning, lately. And that there are a lot of people watching, but they don't seem to see it. Or care?"

"I care. But I know you." When he raises an eyebrow, it seems to add, *And I've fucked you*. I drag a hand across my face as we share a laugh. "We just have to tell them what they don't know."

I start my reply half a dozen times and then shake my head.

"I don't know how to tell this story. There's so much. Nobody would believe me. There are things about this that I still don't even understand."

"What about me? What would you tell me, if there was only one thing you could tell me about all of this. If you knew when you said it that I would believe you?"

I wet my lips, letting my gaze drift across the half-empty club and watching a guy haul an amp across the stage.

"Demeter Bauer is lying to everyone. She poisoned the crops to line her pockets. And I can prove it."

When I dare to look back at him, his eyes are dancing with pride. "Then that's what you'll say."

"To who?" I laugh. "Not everyone is as trusting as you."

"Hermes is," he counters. "And you underestimate how many people trust HMZ."

I drop my gaze to my glass. "Hades doesn't trust him."

"Did he ever say why?"

"No," I offer. *But I bet Juno knows.*

"I don't mean to cross boundaries, Your Highness. But if you've got a message you want to spread, he's the one to help you do it. And if I had to guess, you could practically name your price. Yours is a story everyone wants."

A few notes of an opening melody drift through the space as the evening's musical act warms up, and I give Adonis an uncertain shrug.

"Maybe."

I nurse my wine as the long-haired musician positions himself on a small stool. Someone is adjusting the stage lights, and they shift from blue to green to purple as the guy strums. Something about him is so familiar: the easy posture, the stringed instrument, and the way his hands drift effortlessly across it. Realization dawns.

"Is that...?" I begin.

"Orpheus," Adonis confirms. He points to the willowy brunette lingering at the edge of the stage, leaning closer so I can follow his trajectory. "And his wife."

Chills run down my arms, and I attempt to rub them away until I'm practically hugging myself. My throat is knotted so that I find it hard to breathe, to swallow, to speak. Eventually, I stammer, hoping it can prompt the explanation I so desperately need.

"I brought you here so that you might remember how much *power* lies in your compassion. And also, because the music here is really fucking good. And because that server?" He tosses a glance across the bar. "He totally wants me."

I laugh through the threat of tears, sinking my head against his shoulder.

"Thank you," I say.

He loops his arm around me, hugging me tight.

"I'm glad you're thanking me now, because you'll be cursing me tomorrow."

"Why's that?"

"The hangover," he chortles, clicking his glass to mine. "Drink up, my lady. I feel like you deserve a proper night out."

"You know what?" I muse. "I feel like you're right."

I awake to my head pounding. Actually, no, I awake to *someone* pounding. My door rattles with the force of it. It's a sound that echoes through my apartment as I blink open eyes, dry from yesterday's mascara.

"Seph!" I hear. "Sephie! Are you there?"

I drag myself out of bed and land against the end table with a thud. Pain sears through my hip, slightly sharper than the dull ache in my head. When I open the door, I'm squinting into the daylight. Espe laughs when she sees my face.

"So, it's true, then."

"What's true?"

"You blew us off to stay out all night with *Adonis*," she says, sweeping past me. "Or at least, last night's makeup says it's true."

She seems delighted by this.

"No," I grimace. "I mean, yes. But he's a friend. We're just..."

"Don't worry," she laughs. "I wouldn't insult you by believing *everything* I hear on the news. Unless he's here now. Is he?"

She peers around excitedly.

"No."

The way she deflates is almost comical. "Oh. Well. You want coffee?"

I curl into the corner of my couch and close my eyes, while she moves into my kitchen. "Yes, please."

By the time I hear the machine gurgling and smell the roasted scent of morning, I have the wherewithal to wonder aloud, "If you're not here to interrogate me about Adonis, why are you banging on my door first thing in the morning?"

"I'm banging on your door at two p.m.," she clarifies. "I just got off shift. I had to come tell you."

"Tell me what?"

She dips her hand into her scrub pocket and tosses something across the room at me. Given my current motor skills—or lack thereof—it hits me in the cheek and bounces down my chest.

"Hey!" I protest.

She's still smiling when I dig the hard object from the spot where it rolled between the couch cushions. The moment it's in my hands, my whole body breaks out in goosebumps. My vision blurs with the threat of tears, but I would know the perfectly reddish-purple skin of a radish anywhere. I press it to my nose, sucking in the faint scent of earth and sulfur.

"Where...?" I stammer.

The proud glimmer in her eyes tells me before she does. She points an index finger up, following it with her eyes.

"No," I say.

"Yes!"

I throw the blanket off of myself with a shriek, nearly tackling her with a hug. I bury my face in her hair, and I don't care that she still has that slightly antiseptic aroma that she complains 'smells like hospital.'

She wraps her arms around me, swaying me side to side. "We're back in business, baby!"

19

It turns out, on this side of the river, Juno really is a family counselor. When I convince her to meet me for coffee between sessions, she's wearing an approachable pantsuit and peacock-printed heels. I wait for her to wrap both hands around the oversized mug and take a slow sip of her latte, while I roll my many questions around in my head.

"How've you been?" I venture.

The last time I sat at a cafe with her, we were eating spanakopita in the open air with warm breezes coming off the river Styx. This morning feels similar. The sun is soft. The planters lining the patio are filled with dewy, morning blooms, as if the recent weeks of humid, everyday showers did indeed bring this season's burst of flowers. But of course, my favorite person is missing. I wonder if she feels his absence, too. Wonder if she's seen him lately. Wonder if she knows why he hasn't tried to contact me.

"I don't know what you really came here to ask," she says, interrupting my spiraling thoughts, "but you might as well spill it."

I hate being called out like this, but I know it's no use pretending otherwise.

"Tell me what happened with Hades and Hermes."

Juno sighs in a way that sounds utterly disappointed. Whether it's my asking or her considering it, I can't be sure.

"I really shouldn't be the one telling you this," she says.

"And that's going to stop you?" I tease.

She gives me a stubborn smirk before sinking into confidential sobriety.

"Hades and Zefs go way back, you know. We all do, really. We like to think of it as the beginning—back in the fraternity days, with the core group of us, making our big plans, young enough to still feel like we were on top of the world—but by the time I met him, Zefs had a child from a previous relationship, and that child was Hermes."

I furrow my brow. "You're his step mother?"

"Only in the most general manner of speaking. I love Hermes like a son, but I was never a mother to him, really. He had his own mother, his own life. But later on, he used Zef's connections to work out an arrangement with

Hades. They agreed years ago that Hermes would guide souls to the Styx when it was their time.

"It was a good arrangement for a while. Hermes loved seeing everyone to the border—and getting the scoop from people on their way to cross over, having them confess all their mortal sins, what have you—but Hermes is Hermes. He can't keep his mouth shut. The secrets he gained from this side gig gave him everything he needed to launch HMZ."

"Clever," I murmur.

"Quite," Juno agrees. "The problem is that Hermes wasn't clever enough to not get cocky about it. A few years ago, he announced that he had been the one guiding souls to the ferry and that it was him—and not Hades—who really held the power. The way he told it, he had taken up the job because souls were getting lost and Hades didn't care if they were left to wander for eternity."

"Oh no," I say.

"Oh yes. People started worshiping him in a sense. An entire cult popped up, if you can believe it. He should have discouraged it, but naturally, he ate it up."

"A cult," I repeat. "How did I miss this?"

She waves a hand. "It's basically ancient history at this point. Zefs threatened to disown him, had him shut it down. It was a whole thing. Anyway, the point is that

Hermes... *might* have invited Hades over for an interview and then broached the topic on a live broadcast."

I grimace. "It was bad?"

"You know Hades. He isn't particularly vain or territorial – hell, he's eons more level headed than Zefs – but he actually does care about people, even though many of them by that point had already stopped regarding him as something that concerned them. The waning popularity never seemed to bother him. But how quickly everyone bought into the idea that he didn't care about anyone in the afterlife? He won't readily admit it, but it hurt him. And it solidified his distaste in the things that happen across the river. It created such a strong delineation for him—here, there—and he's held onto it ever since. Or, until you, at least."

"I dunno. I think he's still holding to it," I admit. "I haven't gotten a single message from him since I left."

Juno places a warm hand over mine, her features softening.

"It's not you. He's worried what Hermes will get his hands on. He's got dirt on all the right people, so he sees and hears every message that crosses between here and there. If Hades didn't give you a way to contact him, it's because he's trying to protect you."

If it's true that Hermes is privy to every message that crosses the river, then he should already know there's something deceitful about this entire endeavor, and he hasn't reported on it. Maybe he's been paid off. Or maybe he doesn't yet know how to connect the pieces between me, my mother, and everything that happened over the winter. Everything that's happening still.

"Who said I need to be protected?" I argue.

"You're playing a big game, and a lot of us are worried for you," Juno says gently. "And Hades… well, he worries in more ways than one."

"What ways?"

She sighs. "You know him better than I do, so I know you're aware he worries that he is only capable of ruining things. He wants to give you space to live your own life, make your own choices, and I think it stands to reason that he also worries, if he reaches out to you, that he's coercing you somehow. It's that old 'if you love something, let it go' mentality."

"That's ridiculous," I protest. "I was always his. He didn't have to let me go to figure that out."

"Well, if you want to be able to argue with him about it any time soon, you better win this. It's the only way you'll be able to go back and live your life. Live with *yourself*."

A server drifts past, collecting empty mugs and saucers from a nearby table. I take a few long sips of my now lukewarm coffee, watching until she retreats inside. I swell with a breath.

"You're telling me to trust Hermes."

"I'm not telling you to trust him, I'm telling you to *talk* to him," Juno says. "Just offer him the truth in exchange for escorting you to the river. He won't be able to resist."

20

I write down every sordid detail—about my whirlwind romance, the real source of the blight, my mother's involvement—and seal it in an envelope, leaving it with Espe in case anything happens and Hermes betrays me. It takes so long my hand aches, turns into so many pages that the envelope will barely seal. She tucks the bloated rectangle into a dresser drawer for safe keeping.

Then I ask her to help me dye my hair a temporary shade of deep, dark purple. Her whole kitchen reeks with the chemical smell of it, and when we're done, I tousle my long locks and smile, noting that my loose curls are the color of blooming heliotrope and that they smell as soft and vanilla as the petals.

"It'll come out in three washes," Espe assures me, reading the bottle.

I hold her tight. "I hope everything we've done will last for a lot longer than that."

She squeezes me back. "I hope so, too."

The next morning, I meet with my garden leaders from Bounty and finally show them what we've been doing. They wander around the plants on the rooftop in awe, touching leaves and taking notes. Our seedlings have thrived with the warmer weather, hinting at flourishing crops as we creep towards summer.

Georgio drifts up beside me, surveying the scene with his typical reserved demeanor. He's one of my longest tenured employees, who helped me set up the very first neighborhood garden years ago. His collected calm seemed to anchor the chaos of those early efforts, keeping me grounded when the entire project felt ready to spiral out of control. He strokes his chin in that same way now.

"What do you think?" I ask.

My tone betrays how much their opinions mean to me. I want them to be as excited about this as I am. I *need* them to be.

"I'm hurt you didn't trust us with this." My chest twists with guilt, but his eyes twinkle with forgiveness. "But... I understand, I think."

A butterfly gently alights on a nearby tomato plant, sunning its wings.

"I trust you to make this new business model work," I say. "You'll have to do more with less for a while. Rely on the community. You can't take anything from Big Farma. But Bounty can thrive again. It can do what we set out to do – empower people, teach them, feed them."

Georgio nods, pensive and hopeful.

"What about you?" he asks.

"Oh," I offer wistfully. "I'm sure I'll wash up somewhere."

"The other side of the Styx, perhaps?"

My face goes hot for a moment. This man is old enough to be my father—or grandfather—and knowing that he *knows* everything that goes on over there dredges up that old feeling of shame.

"We all figured you weren't emailing us from the coast of Italy," he offers conspiratorially. "But you seemed... different. Happy."

I bite into my smile. "I was."

He nods. "To happiness, then. Life's certainly too short to settle for less. And we never know where we might find it. Sometimes the most unlikely places. But oh, the bounty they can bring."

That last line tingles across my arms, and I smile, remembering how much happiness we cultivated in that abandoned alley that became the home of our first community garden. *Not enough light*, people said. *Not enough space,* others tutted. *You really think you can* grow *something here? You really think anyone will care?*

But we did. And they did. So many people cared. So many care still.

Our satisfaction simmers. We stand for a while longer at the edge of the rooftop planters, the same way we spent so many mornings over the past few years lingering among tidy rows in back alley gardens, surveying our progress, marinating in the possibilities of everything to come.

With another gentle flap of wings, the visiting butterfly takes flight, leaving the thriving plant behind as it dances into the soft light of morning.

HMZ's headquarters is located in a towering, art deco style building near downtown, with the unmistakable caduceus symbol emblazoned above the row of revolving doors. I have Espe drop me around the corner, and I walk the remaining block with sweat pricking the back of my neck, either from the heat of the day, my rattling nerves, or both. The receptionist doesn't look up from typing as I state my purpose.

"I'm here to see Hermes."

"Do you have an appointment?"

"No."

"Then, no."

I give him a patient smile. "It's important."

"Everybody wants to see Hermes," he drones, "and everybody says it's important."

My eyes slide closed in frustration. I didn't want to have to do this—wield my name like some sort of weapon, the way I've seen my mother do my entire life—but it's all I've got.

"Well," I offer. "Not everybody is Persephone Bauer."

For the first time, his gaze lifts from the screen in front of him. Disbelief is etched into his features. The next time his mouth opens, no words come out.

"Is he available?" I prompt.

The receptionist stammers, then starts speaking in quiet and urgent tones into his headset. After a few seconds, the door to our right buzzes. He gestures nervously.

"He will see you now."

"Awesome," I say, turning on my heel so that the marble floor squeaks.

"Take the elevators to the fourth floor," he calls after me. "His secretary will—"

I raise a hand, not bothering to look back.

"Got it. Thanks."

On the elevator, I press the button as indicated, wondering who puts his office on the fourth floor when this building has fifty stories. I wonder if I'm being sent on a goose chase, or straight into some security holding area, but sure enough, when the doors slide open, I'm met with an oversized, nude statue of Hermes set in the middle of a fountain and a frazzled looking secretary positioned at the desk nearby. The double doors behind her are already opening, and the man himself is stepping out with a broad smile.

His tightly curled, bleached blonde hair reminds me of an uncooked pack of ramen noodles. His outfit is equally ridiculous: an oversized sweater (in the heat of early summer), black leather bottoms that could be pants or leggings, and bright gold high-top sneakers adorned with large wings on either side of each ankle.

"They told me Hades's little pet had finally come to see me, and I told them there was *no way* she would ever set foot in my office, but holy shit—it's really you," he laughs, perching on the edge of the secretary's desk. "I like what you've done with the hair."

The mention of me as 'Hades's little pet' sends ice through my veins. I affect a tone of lethal nonchalance.

"Hello, Hermes. Let's not play games, shall we?"

"All right," he agrees, clearly amused. "Are you going to tell me why you're here?"

"I'm here to tell you about the real source of the blight and Big Farma's involvement in it."

His eyes practically sparkle as he studies me. "There's only one problem with this plan, Persey B. You're not authorized to speak on behalf of Demeter Bauer or her company."

"I don't need authorization."

He tilts his head like a curious dog, all ears.

"And why's that?"

"Because this isn't her story. It's mine."

"Mmm. And you want to tell *me*? Sounds like a risky gamble."

"Should be right up your alley, then."

Hermes hops off the desk and motions me into his office, which looks more like a college fraternity house's fantasy setup than an office workspace. A circular stretch of leather sofas surrounds a game area, with some shoot-em-up multiplayer paused on the big screen. In the corner, there's a bubbling jacuzzi tub. He makes a beeline for the fully stocked bar, which is decorated with a garland made of neon fuzzy dice. It sways as he scoots around the counter to pour himself a drink from a tall glass pitcher.

"Mojito?" he asks.

"No, thanks."

He narrows his eyes at me in amusement, garnishing the rim of his glass with a lime wedge and grabbing a gold swizzle stick topped with a pair of wings. When he stirs it into his drink, the ice clinks.

"Say I hear you out. Spread your message. What is it that you want in return, hm?" he asks, watching me over the rim of his highball glass. "To clear your beloved captor's name? Because I make no promises once I have your story as to how I spin it."

"I want you to escort me to the river Styx. That's how this works, right? You get the scoop, and souls get safe passage? Or did you make that story up, too?"

He narrows his eyes. There's a long moment where I'm sure he won't accept the challenge, but his ego gets the better of him.

"All right, Persey B. You've got yourself a deal." He plops down onto the oversized sofa and motions to the seat across from him. "Ready to roll the dice?"

I wonder if, after all this time, I'm still feeling like the girl who can get everything she wants. If I'm still *lucky*. If good things are still ahead of me. I sink into the sofa and tuck my legs underneath me, knowing there's only one way to find out.

I wet my lips, fingering the delicate gold chain at my collarbone.

"It started with a coin."

27

21

Hints of bergamot and ginger and the woods at dusk mingle in my lungs, teasing my senses and warming my soul as the sun sinks into the river behind me. Like many others stepping off the ferry, the top half of my face is obscured with an ornate mask, tied beneath my dark hair. I slip off my shoes the second I'm inside the palace, longing to feel the warm limestone beneath my feet.

It feels like coming home.

I notice all the ways it feels the same, and in that moment, I simultaneously feel all the ways that I am different. While the partygoers are a flurry of laughter and conversation, I drift quietly into the noise and lights of the atrium and realize I am not the girl I was when I first set foot on this side of the river. I'm not the girl who was last here, either.

Truthfully, I know I haven't changed the world. I'm honest enough to admit that these things follow a familiar pattern. When the news of Demeter's coercion breaks, many people will scoff at the truth and write off Big Farma's manufactured famine as a wild conspiracy. Some will undoubtedly vilify my mother, but the public outrage is only likely to last until the grocery shelves start filling up and something else comes along to demand their attention. Big Farma may lose their government backing and the blank check they've been given to produce new poisons without any red tape, but they'll deny all involvement in the so-called scandal, and in the end they'll walk away clean, the way powerful companies always seem to do.

I also suspect that years from now, when people tell my story, they may still whisper of the Underworld, and kidnapping, and a long, bleak winter. They are likely to gloss over the ugly truths and forget the sacrifices so many made. And they will never know that in this moment, as I return to Hades's palace across the river, that I'm here with my heart on the line.

I cannot ignore the way it thuds in my throat as I drift towards the bar. When I pass the people lounging naked on the sofas or taking their pleasure from each other in the terraced pits, I'm terrified he'll be among them. And yet, all I want is to see him. But I'm not sure I want him to see me just yet.

What if he has forgotten me?

What if in these months I've been away, he realized it was only infatuation, feeble and fleeting?

What if he found someone else?

It's an anxious loop that swirls in my head the same way I circle the dark, decadent wine in my glass a few times before taking a steadying sip. I almost moan as it touches my tongue, because I've missed this. It's true: everything's better here. The sex. The food. The absolute pleasure of existing. I close my eyes with a smile as sweet reminiscence laces my veins. When I reopen them, my gaze snags on him.

It's really him.

He's draped across one of the circular sofas in that cat-like way of his, watching the trio in front of him undress each other. My heart dips into my stomach, wondering if I'm about to see him join them. But the longer I watch him, the more I see how uninterested he is. I bite my bottom lip, attempting to quell my satisfied smirk.

My sweet, disappointed Hades.

When he glances my direction, I drop my gaze quickly. When I dare to look back up, he's watching the group again. The sinking feeling returns, because he didn't recognize me.

Then again, why would he? I dyed my hair and covered my face and wore a cloak over my clothes specifically so he *wouldn't* recognize me. I know it's silly, playing games like this, but I suppose I want some sort of proof. Proof of what, I don't know. That he missed me? That our love was so rare and special that he'd been sitting here, pining for me? That we really were inevitable. Written in the fucking stars.

The server interrupts with a clearing of her throat.

"You've been invited to join a group," she says.

I follow her gesture to the very lounge where Hades is positioned. My heart leaps.

He noticed me.

I give her a small nod of thanks before climbing off my stool and making my way over. I don't walk, I float. My hips sway seductively. My steps feel sexy and sure. Hades motions me into the seat beside him. I've opened my mouth to say something teasing to him when he says, "Tell me your name, darling."

Falling. I think I'm falling. Being sucked into some alternate universe, or turned inside out. I blink at the sudden lack of air, as if the words were a gut punch.

I did this to myself. I know I did. But it doesn't soften the blow.

When I don't reply he purrs, "That's okay. We don't have to talk. I assume you came here for another reason."

I want to recoil when his hand slides up my neck. I'm fighting back the sting of tears when his grip tightens to hold my chin in place. He drags his lips across my jaw. His mouth finds my ear.

"You thought you could sneak back in without me noticing it was you, little nymph?"

A hiccupping gasp escapes me. I want to laugh. I could easily cry. My lips part as he tightens his grip, and I melt into his touch.

"Hades, I—"

"You think your face and your hair and your clothes are the only way I know you from anyone else?" he growls. "I know the way you move. The way you smell. I can feel your energy all the way across the room. But I distinctly remember that we agreed not to hide from each other."

His free hand slips into my hair, and the ribbon loosens, letting the mask fall from my face. When he drags his nose across mine, I whimper.

"I'm sorry. You never called. I wasn't sure if you—"

His lips find mine, and all the certainty I need is in his kiss. I groan against his mouth, letting my fingers trail up his forearms, along his soft shirtsleeves, gripping fistfuls of his hair.

"You weren't sure if I was still yours?" he questions, nipping my bottom lip. "If you were still mine?"

"Yes," I breathe.

He tsk-tsks, tugging the tie of my cape free, letting it slide over my shoulders and pool around us.

"Maybe I need to make you sure, then."

In another quick motion, he snags the front of my shirt and pulls it open until the buttons snap, one after another. My crowded breasts rapidly rise and fall with my breath, and he palms them with a tight squeeze.

"*Oh*," I sigh. "Yes."

One of his hands slides up to surround the column of my throat. He fingers my pulse point. My nipples pinch, turning into hard peaks that press against the lace of my balconette bra, because I want his hands everywhere, all over me.

His eyes are dark pools of lust when they meet mine. "Yes, what?"

"Yes, sir."

"Good girl," he purrs. "You remember the rules."

The whole world slips away when his lips find mine. My entire universe reduces to the immediate space around us, ends at the periphery of me and him. The feel of my bare back against the soft velvet of the sofa. The heat of his body as he hovers over me. The wet warmth of his mouth against my breasts, the sharp tug of his teeth against my nipples.

"Take your fucking pants off, princess."

I shimmy them down over my hips as best I can, and he roughly tugs them the rest of the way down, taking my panties with them. His fingers dip into the slick heat of me, and my eyes roll closed with a moan.

"You weren't sure," he says, rubbing my clit with his thumb as he stretches me around a second finger, a third. "That this wet pussy was still mine?"

My insides clench around him with aching need.

"It's yours," I pant. "I'm yours."

He hooks against my g-spot, massaging roughly. "You're sure?"

"Yes," I moan. "Sir."

He removes his touch too quickly, and I protest before I can catch myself. The "wait, please, stay" has already been uttered. His smile is devilish as he tugs me upright, catching my mouth against his.

"I see you're still the same greedy little slut you were when you left. And I think I need to remind you what happens when you forget yourself."

He bends me over his lap, smoothing his hand up the back of my thigh, along the curve of my backside. I roll my hips against his touch, inching my ass higher, desperate for his caress even under the threat of punishment.

"You know I could put you back on the altar," he says, running his knuckle up and down along my opening. "Tie you up and make you take every single cock in this palace."

I whimper.

"Is that what you want?"

My mind is black with lust, and I find myself leaning further into his touch. Suddenly, a sharp slap lands across my ass, and I yelp.

"Answer the question, little nymph. What is it that you want?"

Heat rushes into my backside, up my neck, into my cheeks.

"I want you."

He spanks me again, harder. "What was that? I couldn't hear you."

"You!" I gasp. Another sting lands across my skin. He strikes me in a quick, sharp series of stinging blows, until my ass is throbbing and numb, until I'm chanting nonsense words and begging for him to understand. "I only want you! I want you so fucking much."

As quickly as the pain began, he shifts me off of his lap, leaving me propped on my knees with my ass in the air and my tear-streaked cheek pressed into the cushions. The sweet relief of his mouth nuzzles between my thighs.

"Oh my god," I breathe.

I shift back to meet his teasing tongue.

"You taste even better than I remember," he murmurs.

He sucks and licks at my sensitive, swollen clit like a ripe fruit, the kind that is so sweet that he can't help letting the juices run down his chin. It's only now, with my face pressed against the sofa, that I realize people are watching us as my pleasure builds. I close my eyes, slipping back into our own private world.

It feels like a dream. A luxurious, lust-filled dream I've had a hundred times since leaving here, wondering if it would ever be real again.

"Fuck, I missed you," I say, emotion choking my voice.

"I missed you, princess." He nuzzles against me again. "Missed your sweet pussy. Missed your dirty mouth. Can you still come for me?"

He massages the heat between my legs, hard and possessive.

"On your cock," I breathe. "Please."

"You know the rules," he taunts. "First, I get what I want. Then you get what you want. And I want to worship your greedy cunt until you're begging me to stop."

I sink my teeth into my bottom lip, furrowing my brow, digging my fingers into the furniture. I rock my hips against his touch, chasing my own pleasure in a way that makes him swear.

"*Fuck*, Persephone. I've thought about this every single day. The way you feel. The way you move. The fucking sounds you make."

Heat spreads, drawing me closer to the edge, and I'm moaning with every breath. He bites the back of my thigh, dipping his fingers into me, letting me ride his hand while he rubs my clit. Release comes hard and fast.

"God, I need you. *Please*."

I hear his zipper, and I nearly sob when I feel the thick head of his cock against my entrance. He runs a hand down the small of my back, spreading it wide around my hip, holding me in place so I can't shift back against him and take him inside me.

"You know I love it when you beg," he says.

"Please fuck me," I whimper.

He rubs himself up and down my slit until I'm trembling.

"Please fuck you?" he teases. "Have you remembered that you're mine, yet?"

"Yes, sir. I'm yours. I'm—"

He presses inside me, stretching me around him, and the rest of my words are lost to my cries of pleasure.

"*Oh.*"

He sinks all the way to the hilt, swearing as my pussy pulses around him. I'm still sensitive from my first orgasm, and when he moves, another fresh wave of wanting spreads through me. He guides my hips back against him again. And again.

"I love you so fucking much, Persephone. I'm never letting you leave again." His voice is thick with desire. His thrusts, possessive. "I don't care if I have to tie you up. Hold you hostage. Make you my goddamn sex slave. Do you understand me, princess?"

"Yes," I breathe.

Each stroke surges through me like an affirmation.

"I am never—"

Yes.

"—letting you—"

Yes.

"—go."

My pleasure crests. I scream his name with every pulsing wave of it, and he fucks me harder to draw it out, until I'm not sure if it will ever stop, until he's filling me up with his own release.

It feels so good. Impossibly good. The kind of sensation that begs to be basked in.

Hades lingers inside me as if he can't bear the idea of being apart. He wraps his arms around me, tugging my back to meet his chest and his mouth to meet the nape of my neck.

"Hades," I breathe.

"Are you really here?" he murmurs against my ear.

His hands rove up the front of my body, teasing my oversensitive skin in absolute reverence. One hand dips between my legs, spreading his fingers wide to feel the place where we're still joined. The other slides possessively over my breasts, up the column of my throat, mimicking the gentle pressure of the collar he placed on me that night which feels like an entire lifetime ago, when he first claimed me as his.

I tip my sweaty face to meet his. "Yes."

He withdraws before settling me across his lap, giving no regard to the hot, slippery spend now coating our thighs.

"How long?"

There's desperation in his voice, betraying the agony of these months we've been apart. My soft reply meets his lips.

"Forever."

"Forever," he hums.

Hades savors the word as if it's something he can taste. When his tongue dips into my mouth, it's like we're trading it back and forth until it's a warm, melty promise.

I brush my nose against his, meeting the midnight ocean of his eyes, his pupils so dark I could drown in them.

"It's a deal, then?"

He holds me tighter against him. His smirk is devious as he drags it against my neck, kissing my pulse point, grazing his mouth beneath my ear. His exhale tingles through me.

"It's an excellent start."

ACKNOWLEDGEMENTS

Writing is often a solo endeavor, but it truly takes a team to bring a book to life. This one would not have been possible without the enthusiasm and support of so many lovely people.

My husband, who continually encourages my writing, sparks my passion, and makes me believe in deep, lasting, someone-should-write-stories-about-this love.

My friend and editor, Jayné, who chatted with me about our Hades + Persephone retelling wish list until I was convinced this book needed to exist, and whose keen insights helped me polish this project into the "smutty unicorn" it is today.

My early readers and moral supporters Kate, Josie, Heather, and Kristen, who boosted my spirits, offered valuable feedback, and could always be counted on to like and share my silly social media posts even when I had zero followers.

And of course you, reader. The world is full of so many amazing books, and I'm grateful that you chose to take a chance on a new author and spend time with this one.

From the bottom of my heart, thank you for sharing this journey with me.

About the Author

January Foxx writes dark, sexy, seductive love stories. She lives with her husband in Memphis, Tennessee.

Stay in the know! Join January's mailing list to get early access to information about future releases, ARC opportunities, exclusive bonus content, and more.